"This is going to sound crazy . . ."

"Joanna," Bobbie said, "I think there's something *here*. In Stepford. It's possible, isn't it? All those fancy plants on Route Nine—electronics, computers, aerospace junk, with Stepford Creek running right behind them—who knows *what* kind of crap they're dumping into the environment."

"What do you *mean*?" Joanna said.

"Just think for a minute," Bobbie said. She fisted her free hand and stuck out a pinky. "Charmaine's changed and become a hausfrau," she said. She stuck out her ring finger. "The woman you spoke to, the one who was president of the women's club; *she* changed, didn't she, from what she must have been before?"

Joanna nodded.

Bobbie's next finger flicked out. "The woman Charmaine played tennis with, before you; she changed too, Charmaine said so."

Joanna frowned. "You think it's—because of a *chemical*?" she said.

Bantam Books by Ira Levin

SLIVER
THE BOYS FROM BRAZIL
THE STEPFORD WIVES
THIS PERFECT DAY
ROSEMARY'S BABY

The Stepford Wives

IRA LEVIN

BANTAM BOOKS
New York Toronto London Sydney Auckland

*This edition contains the complete text
of the original hardcover edition.
Not one word has been omitted.*

*THE STEPFORD WIVES
A Bantam Book / published by arrangement
with Random House*

PRINTING HISTORY
*Random House edition published September 1972.
Bantam edition / March 1991*

ISBN 0-553-29003-7

PUBLISHED SIMULTANEOUSLY IN THE UNITED STATES AND CANADA

*Bantam Books are published by Bantam Books, a division of Bantam Doubleday Dell
Publishing Group, Inc. Its trademark, consisting of the words "Bantam Books" and
the portrayal of a rooster, is Registered in U.S. Patent and Trademark Office and in
other countries. Marca Registrada. Bantam Books, 666 Fifth Avenue, New York,
New York 10103.*

PRINTED IN THE UNITED STATES OF AMERICA

OPM   0 9 8 7 6 5 4 3 2 1

"*Today the combat takes a different shape; instead of wishing to put man in a prison, woman endeavors to escape from one; she no longer seeks to drag him into the realms of immanence but to emerge, herself, into the light of transcendence. Now the attitude of the males creates a new conflict: it is with a bad grace that the man lets her go.*"

—*SIMONE DE BEAUVOIR*
The Second Sex

1

The Welcome Wagon lady, sixty if she was a day but working at youth and vivacity (ginger hair, red lips, a sunshine-yellow dress), twinkled her eyes and teeth at Joanna and said, "You're really going to like it here! It's a nice town with nice people! You couldn't have made a better choice!" Her brown leather shoulder-bag was enormous, old and scuffed; from it she dealt Joanna packets of powdered breakfast drink and soup mix, a toy-size box of non-polluting detergent, a booklet of discount slips good at twenty-two local shops, two cakes of soap, a folder of deodorant pads—

"Enough, enough," Joanna said, standing in the doorway with both hands full. "Hold. Halt. Thank you."

The Welcome Wagon lady put a vial of cologne on

top of the other things, and then searched in her bag
—"No, really," Joanna said—and brought out pink-
framed eyeglasses and a small embroidered notebook.
"I do the 'Notes on Newcomers,'" she said, smiling
and putting on the glasses. "For the *Chronicle*." She
dug at the bag's bottom and came up with a pen,
clicking its top with a red-nailed thumb.

Joanna told her where she and Walter had moved
from; what Walter did and with which firm; Pete's
and Kim's names and ages; what she had done before
they were born; and which colleges she and Walter
had gone to. She shifted impatiently as she spoke,
standing there at the front door with both hands full
and Pete and Kim out of earshot.

"Do you have any hobbies or special interests?"

She was about to say a time-saving no, but hesitated: a full answer, printed in the local paper, might
serve as a signpost to women like herself, potential
friends. The women she had met in the past few days,
the ones in the nearby houses, were pleasant and
helpful enough, but they seemed completely ab-
sorbed in their household duties. Maybe when she
got to know them better she would find they had far-
ther-reaching thoughts and concerns, yet it might be
wise to put up that signpost. So, "Yes, several," she
said. "I play tennis whenever I get the chance, and
I'm a semi-professional photographer—"

"Oh?" the Welcome Wagon lady said, writing.

Joanna smiled. "That means an agency handles
three of my pictures," she said. "And I'm interested
in politics and in the Women's Liberation movement.
Very much so in that. And so is my husband."

"*He* is?" The Welcome Wagon lady looked at her.

"Yes," Joanna said. "Lots of men are." She didn't go into the benefits-for-both-sexes explanation; instead she leaned her head back into the entrance hall and listened: a TV audience laughed in the family room, and Pete and Kim argued but below intervention level. She smiled at the Welcome Wagon lady. "He's interested in boating and football too," she said, "and he collects Early American legal documents." Walter's half of the signpost.

The Welcome Wagon lady wrote, and closed her notebook, clicked her pen. "That's just fine, Mrs. Eberhart," she said, smiling and taking her glasses off. "I know you're going to love it here," she said, "and I want to wish you a sincere and hearty 'Welcome to Stepford.' If there's any information I can give you about local shops and services, please feel free to call me; the number's right there on the front of the discount book."

"Thank you, I will," Joanna said. "And thanks for all this."

"Try them, they're good products!" the Welcome Wagon lady said. She turned away. "Good-by now!"

Joanna said good-by to her and watched her go down the curving walk toward her battered red Volkswagen. Dogs suddenly filled its windows, a black and brown excitement of spaniels, jumping and barking, paws pressing glass. Moving whiteness beyond the Volkswagen caught Joanna's eye: across the sapling-lined street, in one of the Claybrooks' upstairs windows, whiteness moved again, leaving one pane and filling the next; the window was being washed. Joanna smiled, in case Donna Claybrook was looking at her. The whiteness moved to a lower pane, and then to the pane beside it.

With a surprising roar the Volkswagen lunged from the curb, and Joanna backed into the entrance hall and hipped the door closed.

Pete and Kim were arguing louder. "B.M.! Diarrhea!" "Ow! Stop it!"

"Cut it out!" Joanna called, dumping the double handful of samples onto the kitchen table.

"She's kicking me!" Pete shouted, and Kim shouted, "I'm not! You diarrhea!"

"Now *stop* it," Joanna said, going to the port and looking through. Pete lay on the floor too close to the TV set, and Kim stood beside him, red-faced, keeping from kicking him. Both were still in their pajamas. "She kicked me twice," Pete said, and Kim shouted, "You changed the channel! He changed the channel!" "I did not!" "*I was watching Felix the Cat!*"

"Quiet!" Joanna commanded. "Absolute silence! Utter—complete—total—silence."

They looked at her, Kim with Walter's wide blue eyes, Pete with her own grave dark ones. "Race 'em to a flying finish!" the TV set cried. "No electricity!"

"A, you're too close to the set," Joanna said. "B, turn it off; and C, get dressed, both of you. That green stuff outside is grass, and the yellow stuff coming down on it is sunshine." Pete scrambled to his feet and powed the TV's control panel, blanking its screen to a dying dot of light. Kim began crying.

Joanna groaned and went around into the family room.

Crouching, she hugged Kim to her shoulder and rubbed her pajamaed back, kissed her silk-soft ringlets. "Ah, come on now," she said. "Don't you want to play with that nice Allison again? Maybe you'll see another chipmunk."

Pete came over and lifted a strand of her hair. She looked up at him and said, "Don't change *channels* on her."

"Oh, all right," he said, winding a finger in the dark strand.

"And don't *kick*," she told Kim. She rubbed her back and tried to get kisses in at her squirming-away cheek.

It was Walter's turn to do the dishes, and Pete and Kim were playing quietly in Pete's room, so she took a quick cool shower and put on shorts and a shirt and her sneakers and brushed her hair. She peeked in on Pete and Kim as she tied her hair: they were sitting on the floor playing with Pete's space station.

She moved quietly away and went down the new-carpeted stairs. It was a good evening. The unpacking was done with, finally, and she was cool and clean, with a few free minutes—ten or fifteen if she was lucky—to maybe sit outside with Walter and look at their trees and their two-point-two acres.

She went around and down the hallway. The kitchen was spick-and-span, the washer pounding. Walter was at the sink, leaning to the window and looking out toward the Van Sant house. A Rorschach-blot of sweat stained his shirt: a rabbit with its ears bent outward. He turned around, and started and smiled. "How long have you been here?" he asked, dishtowel-wiping his hands.

"I just came in," she said.

"You look reborn."

"That's how I feel. They're playing like angels. You want to go outside?"

"Okay," he said, folding the towel. "Just for a few minutes though. I'm going over to talk with Ted." He slid the towel onto a rod of the rack. "That's why I was looking," he said. "They just finished eating."

"What are you going to talk with him about?"

They went out onto the patio.

"I was going to tell you," he said as they walked. "I've changed my mind; I'm joining that Men's Association."

She stopped and looked at him.

"Too many important things are centered there to just opt out of it," he said. "Local politicking, the charity drives and so on . . ."

She said, "How can you join an *outdated, old-fash-ioned—*"

"I spoke to some of the men on the train," he said. "Ted, and Vic Stavros, and a few others they introduced me to. They *agree* that the no-women-allowed business is archaic." He took her arm and they walked on. "But the only way to change it is from inside," he said. "So I'm going to help do it. I'm joining Saturday night. Ted's going to brief me on who's on what committees." He offered her his cigarettes. "Are you smoking or non- tonight?"

"Oh—*smoking*," she said, reaching for one.

They stood at the patio's far edge, in cool blue dusk twanging with crickets, and Walter held his lighter flame to Joanna's cigarette and to his own.

"Look at that sky," he said. "Worth every penny it cost us."

She looked—the sky was mauve and blue and dark blue; lovely—and then she looked at her cigarette. "Organizations can be changed from the outside," she said. "You get up petitions, you picket—"

"But it's easier from the inside," Walter said. "You'll see: if these men I spoke to are typical, it'll be the *Everybody's* Association before you know it. Co-ed poker. Sex on the pool table."

"If these men you spoke to were typical," she said, "it would be the Everybody's Association already. Oh, all right, go ahead and join; I'll think up slogans for placards. I'll have plenty of time when school starts."

He put his arm around her shoulders and said, "Hold off a little while. If it's not open to women in six months, I'll quit and we'll march together. Shoulder to shoulder. 'Sex, yes; sexism, no.' "

" 'Stepford is out of step,' " she said, reaching for the ashtray on the picnic table.

"Not bad."

"Wait till I really get going."

They finished their cigarettes and stood arm in arm, looking at their dark wide runway of lawn, and the tall trees, black against mauve sky, that ended it. Lights shone among the trunks of the trees: windows of houses on the next street over, Harvest Lane.

"Robert Ardrey is right," Joanna said. "I feel very territorial."

Walter looked around at the Van Sant house and then squinted at his watch. "I'm going to go in and wash up," he said, and kissed her cheek.

She turned and took his chin and kissed his lips. "I'm going to stay out a few minutes," she said. "Yell if they're acting up."

"Okay," he said. He went into the house by the living-room door.

She held her arms and rubbed them; the evening was growing cooler. Closing her eyes, she threw her head back and breathed the smell of grass and trees and clean air: delicious. She opened her eyes, to a single speck of star in dark blue sky, a trillion miles above her. "Star light, star bright," she said. She didn't say the rest of it, but she thought it.

She wished—that they would be happy in Stepford. That Pete and Kim would do well in school, and that she and Walter would find good friends and fulfillment. That he wouldn't mind the commuting—though the whole idea of moving had been his in the first place. That the lives of all four of them would be enriched, rather than diminished, as she had feared, by leaving the city—the filthy, crowded, crime-ridden, but so-alive city.

Sound and movement turned her toward the Van Sant house.

Carol Van Sant, a dark silhouette against the radiance of her kitchen doorway, was pressing the lid down onto a garbage can. She bent to the ground, red hair glinting, and came up with something large and round, a stone; she put it on top of the lid.

"Hi!" Joanna called.

Carol straightened and stood facing her, tall and leggy and naked-seeming—but edged by the purple of a lighted-from-behind dress. "Who's there?" she called.

"Joanna Eberhart," Joanna said. "Did I scare you? I'm sorry if I did." She went toward the fence that divided her and Walter's property from the Van Sants'.

"Hi, Joanna," Carol said in her nasal New Englandy voice. "No, you didn't scay-er me. It's a nice night, isn't it?"

"Yes," Joanna said. "And I'm done with my unpacking, which makes it even nicer." She had to speak loud; Carol had stayed by her doorway, still too far away for comfortable conversation even though she herself was now at the flower bed edging the split-rail fence. "Kim had a great time with Allison this afternoon," she said. "They get along beautifully together."

"Kim's a sweet little girl," Carol said. "I'm glad Allison has such a nice new friend next door. Good night, Joanna." She turned to go in.

"Hey, wait a minute!" Joanna called.

Carol turned back. "Yes?" she said.

Joanna wished that the flower bed and fence weren't there, so she could move closer. Or, darn it, that Carol would come to *her* side of the fence. What was so top-priority-urgent in that fluorescent-lighted copper-pot-hanging kitchen? "Walter's coming over to talk with Ted," she said, speaking loud to Carol's naked-seeming silhouette. "When you've got the kids down, why don't you come over and have a cup of coffee with me?"

"Thanks, I'd like to," Carol said, "but I have to wax the family-room floor."

"Tonight?"

"Night is the only time to do it, until school starts."

"Well can't it wait? It's only three more days."

Carol shook her head. "No, I've put it off too long as it is," she said. "It's all over scuff-marks. And besides, Ted will be going to the Men's Association later on."

"Does he go every night?"

"Just about."

Dear God! "And you stay home and do housework?"

"There's always something or other that has to be done," Carol said. "You know how it is. I have to finish the kitchen now. Good night."

"Good night," Joanna said, and watched Carol go —profile of too-big bosom—into her kitchen and close the door. She reappeared almost instantly at the over-the-sink window, adjusting the water lever, taking hold of something and scrubbing it. Her red hair was neat and gleaming; her thin-nosed face looked

thoughtful (and, damn it all, *intelligent*); her big pur-
pled breasts bobbed with her scrubbing.

Joanna went back to the patio. No, she *didn't* know
how it was, thank God. Not to be like that, a compul-
sive hausfrau. Who could blame Ted for taking ad-
vantage of such an asking-to-be-exploited patsy?

She could blame him, that's who.

Walter came out of the house in a light jacket. "I
don't think I'll be more than an hour or so," he said.

"That Carol Van Sant is not to be believed," she
said. "She can't come over for a cup of coffee because
she has to *wax* the *family-room floor*. Ted goes to the
Men's Association every night and *she* stays home doing *housework*."

"Jesus," Walter said, shaking his head.

"Next to *her*," she said, "my mother is Kate Mil-
lett."

He laughed. "See you later," he said, and kissed
her cheek and went away across the patio.

She took another look at her star, brighter now—
Get to work, you, she thought to it—and went into the
house.

The four of them went out together Saturday morning, seatbelted into their spotless new station wagon;
Joanna and Walter in sunglasses, talking of stores and
shopping, and Pete and Kim power-switching their
windows down and up and down and up till Walter
told them to stop it. The day was vivid and gem-

edged, a signal of autumn. They drove to Stepford Center (white frame Colonial shopfronts, postcard pretty) for discount-slip hardware and pharmaceuticals; then south on Route Nine to a large new shopping mall—discount-slip shoes for Pete and Kim (what a wait!) and a no-discount jungle gym; then east on Eastbridge Road to a McDonald's (Big Macs, chocolate shakes); and a little farther east for antiques (an octagonal end table, no documents); and then north-south-east-west all over Stepford—Anvil Road, Cold Creek Road, Hunnicutt, Beavertail, Burgess Ridge— to show Pete and Kim (Joanna and Walter had seen it all house-hunting) their new school and the schools they would go to later on, the you'd-never-guess-what-it-is-from-the-outside non-polluting incinerator plant, and the picnic grounds where a community pool was under construction. Joanna sang "Good Morning Starshine" at Pete's request, and they all did "MacNamara's Band" with each one imitating a different instrument in the final part, and Kim threw up, but with enough warning for Walter to pull over and stop and get her unbuckled and out of the station wagon in time, thank God.

That quieted things down. They drove back through Stepford Center—slowly, because Pete said that *he* might throw up too. Walter pointed out the white frame library, and the Historical Society's two-hundred-year-old white frame cottage.

Kim, looking upward through her window, lifted a sucked-thin Life Saver from her tongue and said, "What's that big one?"

"That's the Men's Association house," Walter said.

Pete leaned to his seatbelt's limit and ducked and looked. "Is that where you're going tonight?" he asked.

"That's right," Walter said.

"How do you get to it?"

"There's a driveway farther up the hill."

They had come up behind a truck with a man in khakis standing in its open back, his arms stretched to its sides. He had brown hair and a long lean face and wore eyeglasses. "That's Gary Claybrook, isn't it?" Joanna said.

Walter pressed a fleeting horn-beep and waved his arm out the window. Their across-the-street neighbor bent to look at them, then smiled and waved and caught hold of the truck. Joanna smiled and waved. Kim yelled, "Hello, Mr. Claybrook!" and Pete yelled, "Where's Jeremy?"

"He can't hear you," Joanna said.

"I wish I could ride a truck that way!" Pete said, and Kim said, "Me too!"

The truck was creeping and grinding, fighting against the steep left-curving upgrade. Gary Claybrook smiled self-consciously at them. The truck was half filled with small cartons.

"What's he doing, moonlighting?" Joanna asked.

"Not if he makes as much as Ted says he does," Walter said.

"Oh?"

"What's moonlighting?" Pete asked.

The truck's brake lights flashed; it stopped, its left-turn signal winking.

Joanna explained what moonlighting was.

A car shot down the hill, and the truck began moving across the left lane. "Is that the driveway?" Pete asked, and Walter nodded and said, "Yep, that's it." Kim switched her window farther down, shouting, "Hello, Mr. Claybrook!" He waved as they drove past him.

Pete sprung his seatbelt buckle and jumped around onto his knees. "Can I go there sometime?" he asked, looking out the back.

"Mm-mmn, sorry," Walter said. "No kids allowed."

"Boy, they've got a great big fence!" Pete said. "Like in *Hogan's Heroes!*"

"To keep women out," Joanna said, looking ahead, a hand to the rim of her sunglasses.

Walter smiled.

"Really?" Pete asked. "Is that what it's for?"

"Pete took his belt off," Kim said.

"Pete—" Joanna said.

They drove up Norwood Road, then west on Winter Hill Drive.

As a matter of principle she wasn't going to do any housework. Not that there wasn't plenty to do, God knows, and some that she actually *wanted* to do, like getting the living-room bookshelves squared away— but not tonight, no sir. It could darn well wait. She wasn't Carol Van Sant and she wasn't Mary Ann

Stavros—pushing a vacuum cleaner past a downstairs window when she went to lower Pete's shade.

No sir. Walter was at the Men's Association, fine; he *had* to go there to join, and he'd have to go there once or twice a week to get it changed. But she wasn't going to do housework while he was there (at least not this first time) any more than *he* was going to do it when *she* was out somewhere—which she was going to be on the next clear moonlit night: down in the Center getting some time exposures of those Colonial shopfronts. (The hardware store's irregular panes would wobble the moon's reflection, maybe interestingly.)

So once Pete and Kim were sound asleep she went down to the cellar and did some measuring and planning in the storage room that was going to be her darkroom, and then she went back up, checked Pete and Kim, and made herself a vodka and tonic and took it into the den. She put the radio on to some schmaltzy but nice Richard-Rodgersy stuff, moved Walter's contracts and things carefully from the center of the desk, and got out her magnifier and red pencil and the contact sheets of her quick-before-I-leave-the-city pictures. Most of them were a waste of film, as she'd suspected when taking them—she was never any good when she was rushing—but she found one that really excited her, a shot of a well-dressed young black man with an attaché case, glaring venomously at an empty cab that had just passed him. If his expression enlarged well, and if she darkened the background to bring up the blurred cab, it could be an arresting picture—one she was sure the agency would be willing to handle. There were plenty of markets for pictures dramatizing racial tensions.

She red-penciled an asterisk beside the print and went on looking for others that were good or at least part good but croppable. She remembered her vodka and tonic and sipped it.

At a quarter past eleven she was tired, so she put her things away in her side of the desk, put Walter's things back where they had been, turned the radio off, and brought her glass into the kitchen and rinsed it. She checked the doors, turned the lights off—except the one in the entrance hall—and went upstairs.

Kim's elephant was on the floor. She picked it up and tucked it under the blanket beside the pillow; then pulled the blanket up onto Kim's shoulders and fondled her ringlets very lightly.

Pete was on his back with his mouth open, exactly as he had been when she had checked before. She waited until she saw his chest move, then opened his door wider, switched the hall light off, and went into her and Walter's room.

She undressed, braided her hair, showered, rubbed in face cream, brushed her teeth, and got into bed.

Twenty of twelve. She turned the lamp off.

Lying on her back, she swung out her right leg and arm. She missed Walter beside her, but the expanse of cool-sheet smoothness was pleasant. How many times had she gone to bed alone since they were married? Not many: the nights he'd been out of town on Marburg-Donlevy business; the times she'd been in the hospital with Pete and Kim; the night of the power failure; when she'd gone home for Uncle Bert's funeral—maybe twenty or twenty-five times in all, in the ten years and a little more. It wasn't a bad feeling. By God, it made her feel like Joanna Ingalls again. Remember her?

She wondered if Walter was getting bombed. That was liquor on that truck that Gary Claybrook had been riding in (or had the cartons been too small for liquor?). But Walter had gone in Vic Stavros's car, so let him get bombed. Not that he really was likely to; he hardly ever did. What if Vic Stavros got bombed? The sharp curves on Norwood Road—

Oh nuts. Why worry?

The bed was shaking. She lay in the dark seeing the darker dark of the open bathroom door, and the glint of the dresser's handles, and the bed kept shaking her in a slow steady rhythm, each shake accompanied by a faint spring-squeak, again and again and again. It was Walter who was shaking! He had a fever! Or the d.t.'s? She spun around and leaned to him on one arm, staring, reaching to find his brow. His eye-whites looked at her and turned instantly away; all of him turned from her, and the tenting of the blanket at his groin was gone as she saw it, replaced by the shape of his hip. The bed became still.

He had been—masturbating?

She didn't know what to say.

She sat up.

"I thought you had the d.t.'s," she said. "Or a fever."

He lay still. "I didn't want to wake you," he said. "It's after two."

She sat there and caught her breath.

He stayed on his side, not saying anything.

She looked at the room, its windows and furniture dim in the glow from the night light in Pete and Kim's bathroom. She fixed her braid down straight and rubbed her hand on her midriff.

"You could have," she said. "Woke me. I wouldn't have minded."

He didn't say anything.

"Gee whiz, you don't have to do *that*," she said.

"I just didn't want to wake you," he said. "You were sound asleep."

"Well next time wake me."

He came over onto his back. No tent.

"Did you?" she asked.

"*No,*" he said.

"Oh," she said. "Well"—and smiled at him—"now I'm up." She lay down beside him, turning to him, and held her arm out over him; and he turned to her and they embraced and kissed. He tasted of Scotch. "I mean, consideration is fine," she said in his ear, "but Jesus."

It turned out to be one of their best times ever—for her, at least. "Wow," she said, coming back from the bathroom, "I'm still weak."

He smiled at her, sitting in bed and smoking.

She got in with him and settled herself comfortably under his arm, drawing his hand down onto her breast. "What did they do," she said, "show you dirty movies or something?"

He smiled. "No such luck," he said. He put his cigarette by her lips, and she took a puff of it. "They took eight-fifty from me in poker," he said, "and they chewed my ear off about the Zoning Board's evil intentions re Eastbridge Road."

"I was afraid you were getting bombed."

"Me? Two Scotches. They're not heavy drinkers. What did *you* do?"

She told him, and about her hopes for the picture of the black man. He told her about some of the men he had met: the pediatrician the Van Sants and the Claybrooks had recommended, the magazine illustrator who was Stepford's major celebrity, two other lawyers, a psychiatrist, the Police Chief, the manager of the Center Market.

"The psychiatrist should be in favor of letting women in," she said.

"He is," Walter said. "And so is Dr. Verry. I didn't sound out any of the others; I didn't want to come on as too much of an activist my first time there."

"When are you going again?" she asked—and was suddenly afraid (why?) that he would say *tomorrow*.

"I don't know," he said. "Listen, I'm not going to make it a way of life the way Ted and Vic do. I'll go in a week or so, I guess; I don't know. It's kind of provincial really."

She smiled and snuggled closer to him.

.   .   .

She was about a third of the way down the stairs,
going by foot-feel, holding the damn laundry basket
to her face because of the damn banister, when
wouldn't you know it, the double-damn phone rang.

She couldn't put the basket down, it would fall,
and there wasn't enough room to turn around with it
and go back up; so she kept going slowly down, foot-
feeling and thinking *Okay, okay* to the phone's an-
swer-me-this-instant ringing.

She made it to the bottom, put the basket down,
and stalked to the den desk.

"Hello," she said—the way she felt, with no put-on
graciousness.

"Hi, is this Joanna Eberhart?" The voice was loud,
happy, raspy; Peggy Clavenger-ish. But Peggy Clav-
enger had been with *Paris-Match* the last she'd heard,
and wouldn't even know she was married, let alone
where she was living.

"Yes," she said. "Who's this?"

"We haven't been formally introduced," the no-
not-Peggy-Clavenger voice said, "but I'm going to do
it right now. Bobbie, I'd like you to meet Joanna
Eberhart. Joanna, I'd like you to meet Bobbie
Markowe—that's *K O W E.* Bobbie has been living
here in Ajax Country for five weeks now, and she'd
like very much to know an 'avid shutterbug with a
keen interest in politics and the Women's Lib movement.' That's you, Joanna, according to what it says

here in the *Stepford Chronicle*. Or *Chronic Ill*, depending on your journalistic standards. Have they conveyed an accurate impression of you? Are you really not deeply concerned about whether pink soap pads are better than blue ones or vice versa? Given complete freedom of choice, would you just as soon *not* squeeze the Charmin? Hello? Are you still there, Joanna? Hello?"

"Hello," Joanna said. "Yes, I'm here. *And how* I'm here! Hello! Son of a gun, it pays to advertise!"

"What a pleasure to see a messy kitchen!" Bobbie said. "It doesn't quite come up to mine—you don't have the little peanut-butter handprints on the cabinets—but it's good, it's very good. Congratulations."

"I can show you some dull dingy bathrooms if you'd like," Joanna said.

"Thanks. I'll just take the coffee."

"Is instant okay?"

"You mean there's something else?"

She was short and heavy-bottomed, in a blue Snoopy sweatshirt and jeans and sandals. Her mouth was big, with unusually white teeth, and she had blue take-in-everything eyes and short dark tufty hair. And small hands and dirty toes. And a husband named Dave who was a stock analyst, and three sons, ten, eight, and six. And an Old English sheepdog and a corgi. She looked a bit younger than Joanna, thirty-two or -three. She drank two cups of coffee and ate a

Ring Ding and told Joanna about the women of Fox
Hollow Lane.

"I'm beginning to think there's a—nationwide
contest I haven't heard about," she said, tonguing her
chocolated fingertips. "A million dollars and—Paul
Newman for the cleanest house by next Christmas. I
mean, it's scrub, scrub, *scrub*; wax, wax, *wax*—"

"It's the same around here," Joanna said. "Even at
night! And the men all—"

"The Men's Association!" Bobbie cried.

They talked about it—the antiquated sexist unfair-
ness of it, the real *injustice*, in a town with no wom-
en's organization, not even a League of Women
Voters. "Believe me, I've combed this place," Bobbie
said. "There's the Garden Club, and a few old-biddy
church groups—for which I'm not eligible anyway;
'Markowe' is upward-mobile for 'Markowitz'—and
there's the very non-sexist Historical Society. Drop
in and say hello to them. Corpses in lifelike posi-
tions."

Dave was in the Men's Association, and like Walter, thought it could be changed from within. But
Bobbie knew better: "You'll see, we'll have to chain
ourselves to the fence before we get any action. How
about that fence? You'd think they were refining
opium!"

They talked about the possibility of having a get-
together with some of their neighbors, a rap session
to wake them to the more active role they could play
in the town's life; but they agreed that the women
they had met seemed unlikely to welcome even so
small a step toward liberation. They talked about the

National Organization for Women, to which they both belonged, and about Joanna's photography.

"My God, these are *great*!" Bobbie said, looking at the four mounted enlargements Joanna had hung in the den. "They're *terrific*!"

Joanna thanked her.

" 'Avid shutterbug'! I thought that meant Polaroids of the kids! These are *marvelous*!"

"Now that Kim's in kindergarten I'm really going to get to work," Joanna said.

She walked Bobbie to her car.

"Damn it, *no*," Bobbie said. "We ought to *try* at least. Let's talk to these hausfraus; there must be *some* of them who resent the situation a little. What do you say? Wouldn't it be great if we could get a group together—maybe even a NOW chapter eventually—and give that Men's Association a good shaking-up? Dave and Walter are kidding themselves; it's not going to change unless it's *forced* to change; fat-cat organizations never do. What do you say, Joanna? Let's ask around."

Joanna nodded. "We should," she said. "They can't all be as content as they seem."

She spoke to Carol Van Sant. "Gee, no, Joanna," Carol said. "That doesn't sound like the sort of thing that would interest me. Thanks for ay-isking me though." She was cleaning the plastic divider in Stacy and Allison's room, wiping a span of its accor-

dion folds with firm downstrokes of a large yellow
sponge.

"It would only be for a couple of hours," Joanna
said. "In the evening, or if it's more convenient for
everybody, sometime during school hours."

Carol, crouching to wipe the lower part of the
span, said, "I'm sorry, but I just don't have much
time for that sort of thing."

Joanna watched her for a moment. "Doesn't it
bother you," she said, "that the central organization
here in Stepford, the *only* organization that does anything significant as far as community projects are
concerned, is off limits to women? Doesn't that seem
a little archaic to you?"

" 'Ar-kay-ic'?" Carol said, squeezing her sponge in
a bucket of sudsy water.

Joanna looked at her. "Out of date, old-fashioned,"
she said.

Carol squeezed the sponge out above the bucket.
"No, it doesn't seem archaic to me," she said. She
stood up straight and reached the sponge to the top of
the next span of folds. "Ted's better equipped for that
sort of thing than I am," she said, and began wiping
the folds with firm downstrokes, each one neatly
overlapping the one before. "And men need a place
where they can relax and have a drink or two," she
said.

"Don't women?"

"No, not as much." Carol shook her neat red-
haired shampoo-commercial head, not turning from
her wiping. "I'm sorry, Joanna," she said, "I just
don't have time for a get-together."

"Okay," Joanna said. "If you change your mind, let me know."

"Would you mind if I don't walk you downstairs?"

"No, of course not."

She spoke to Barbara Chamalian, on the other side of the Van Sants. "Thanks, but I don't see how I could manage it," Barbara said. She was a square-jawed brown-haired woman, in a snug pink dress molding an exceptionally good figure. "Lloyd stays in town a lot," she said, "and the evenings he doesn't, he likes to go to the Men's Association. I'd hate to pay a sitter for just—"

"It could be during school hours," Joanna said.

"No," Barbara said, "I think you'd better count me out." She smiled, widely and attractively. "I'm glad we've met though," she said. "Would you like to come in and sit for a while? I'm ironing."

"No, thanks," Joanna said. "I want to speak to some of the other women."

She spoke to Marge McCormick ("I honestly don't think I'd be interested in that") and Kit Sundersen ("I'm afraid I haven't the time; I'm really sorry, Mrs. Eberhart") and Donna Claybrook ("That's a nice idea, but I'm so busy these days. Thanks for asking me though").

She met Mary Ann Stavros in an aisle in the Center Market. "No, I don't think I'd have time for anything like that. There's so much to do around the house. You know."

"But you go out *sometimes*, don't you?" Joanna said.

"Of course I do," Mary Ann said. "I'm out now, aren't I?"

"I mean *out*. For relaxation."

Mary Ann smiled and shook her head, swaying her sheaves of straight blond hair. "No, not often," she said. "I don't feel much need for relaxation. See you." And she went away, pushing her grocery cart; and stopped, took a can from a shelf, looked at it, and fitted it down into her cart and went on.

Joanna looked after her, and into the cart of another woman going slowly past her. *My God*, she thought, *they even fill their carts neatly!* She looked into her own: a jumble of boxes and cans and jars. A guilty impulse to put it in order prodded her; but *I'm damned if I will!* she thought, and grabbed a box from the shelf—Ivory Snow—and tossed it in. Didn't even need the damn stuff!

She spoke to the mother of one of Kim's classmates in Dr. Verry's waiting room; and to Yvonne Weisgalt, on the other side of the Stavroses; and to Jill Burke, in the next house over. All of them turned her down; they either had too little time or too little interest to meet with other women and talk about their shared experiences.

Bobbie had even worse luck, considering that she spoke to almost twice as many women. "One taker," she told Joanna. "One eighty-five-year-old widow who dragged me through her door and kept me prisoner for a solid hour of close-up saliva spray. Any time we're ready to storm the Men's Association, Eda Mae Hamilton is ready and willing."

"We'd better keep in touch with her," Joanna said.

"Oh no, we're not done yet!"

They spent a morning calling on women together,

on the theory (Bobbie's) that the two of them, speaking in planned ambiguities, might create the encouraging suggestion of a phalanx of women with room for one more. It didn't work.

"Jee-*zus*!" Bobbie said, ramming her car viciously up Short Ridge Hill. "Something *fishy* is going on here! We're in the Town That Time Forgot!"

One afternoon Joanna left Pete and Kim in the care of sixteen-year-old Melinda Stavros and took the train into the city, where she met Walter and their friends Shep and Sylvia Tackover at an Italian restaurant in the theater district. It was good to see Shep and Sylvia again; they were a bright, homely, energetic couple who had survived several bad blows, including the death by drowning of a four-year-old son. It was good to be in the city again too; Joanna relished the color and bustle of the busy restaurant.

She and Walter spoke enthusiastically about Stepford's beauty and quiet, and the advantages of living in a house rather than an apartment. She didn't say anything about how home-centered the Stepford women were, or about the absence of outside-the-home activities. It was vanity, she supposed; an unwillingness to make herself the object of commiseration, even Shep and Sylvia's. She told them about Bobbie and how amusing she was, and about Stepford's fine uncrowded schools. Walter didn't bring up the Men's Association and neither did she. Sylvia, who was with the city's Housing and Development Administration, would have had a fit.

But on the way to the theater Sylvia gave her a sharp appraising look and said, "A tough adjustment?"

"In ways," she said.

"You'll make it," Sylvia said, and smiled at her. "How's the photography? It must be great for you up there, coming to everything with a fresh eye."

"I haven't done a damn thing," she said. "Bobbie and I have been running around trying to drum up some Women's Lib activity. It's a bit of a backwater, to tell the truth."

"Running and drumming isn't your work," Sylvia said. "Photography is, or ought to be."

"I know," she said. "I've got a plumber coming in any day now to put in the darkroom sink."

"Walter looks chipper."

"He is. It's a good life really."

The play, a musical hit of the previous season, was disappointing. In the train going home, after they had hashed it over for a few minutes, Walter put on his glasses and got out some paper work, and Joanna skimmed *Time* and then sat looking out the window and smoking, watching the darkness and the occasional lights riding through it.

Sylvia was right; photography was her work. To hell with the Stepford women. Except Bobbie, of course.

Both cars were at the station, so they had to ride home separately. Joanna went first in the station wagon and Walter followed her in the Toyota. The

Center was empty and stage-setty under its three streetlights—yes, she would take pictures there, *before* the darkroom was finished—and there were headlights and lighted windows up at the Men's Association house, and a car waiting to pull out of its driveway.

Melinda Stavros was yawning but smiling, and Pete and Kim were in their beds sound asleep.

In the family room there were empty milk glasses and plates on the lamp table, and crumpled balls of white paper on the sofa and the floor before it, and an empty ginger-ale bottle on the floor among the balls of paper.

At least they don't pass it on to their daughters, Joanna thought.

The third time Walter went to the Men's Association he called at about nine o'clock and told Joanna he was bringing home the New Projects Committee, to which he had been appointed the time before. Some construction work was being done at the house (she could hear the whine of machinery in the background) and they couldn't find a quiet place where they could sit and talk.

"Fine," she said. "I'm getting the rest of the junk out of the darkroom, so you can have the whole—"

"No, listen," he said, "stay upstairs with us and get into the conversation. A couple of them are die-hard men-only's; it won't do them any harm to hear a

woman make intelligent comments. I'm assuming
you will."

"Thanks. Won't they object?"

"It's our house."

"Are you sure you're not looking for a waitress?"

He laughed. "Oh God, there's no fooling her," he
said. "Okay, you got me. But an intelligent waitress,
all right? Would you? It really might do some good."

"Okay," she said. "Give me fifteen minutes and I'll
even be an intelligent *beautiful* waitress; how's that
for cooperation?"

"Fantastic. Unbelievable."

There were five of them, and one, a cheery little red-
faced man of about sixty, with toothpick-ends of
waxed mustache, was Ike Mazzard, the magazine illustrator. Joanna, shaking his hand warmly, said,
"I'm not sure I like you; you blighted my adolescence
with those dream girls of yours!" And he, chuckling,
said, "You must have matched up pretty well."

"Would you like to bet on that?" she said.

The other four were all late-thirties or early-for-
ties. The tall black-haired one, laxly arrogant, was
Dale Coba, the president of the association. He
smiled at her with green eyes that disparaged her,
and said, "Hello, Joanna, it's a pleasure." *One of the
die-hard men-only's,* she thought; *women are to lay.* His
hand was smooth, without pressure.

The others were Anselm or Axhelm, Sundersen,

Roddenberry. "I met your wife," she said to Sundersen, who was pale and paunchy, nervous-seeming. "If
you're the Sundersens across the way, that is."

"You did? We are, yes. We're the only ones in Stepford."

"I invited her to a get-together, but she couldn't
make it."

"She's not very social." Sundersen's eyes looked
elsewhere, not at her.

"I'm sorry, I missed your first name," she said.

"Herb," he said, looking elsewhere.

She saw them all into the living room and went
into the kitchen for ice and soda, and brought them to
Walter at the bar cabinet. "Intelligent? Beautiful?"
she said, and he grinned at her. She went back into
the kitchen and filled bowls with potato chips and
peanuts.

There were no objections from the circle of men
when, holding her glass, she said "May I?" and eased
into the sofa-end Walter had saved for her. Ike Mazzard and Anselm-or-Axhelm rose, and the others
made I'm-thinking-of-rising movements—except
Dale Coba, who sat eating peanuts out of his fist,
looking across the cocktail table at her with his dis-
paraging green eyes.

They talked about the Christmas-Toys project and
the Preserve-the-Landscape project. Roddenberry's
name was Frank, and he had a pleasant pug-nosed
blue-chinned face and a slight stutter; and Coba had a
nickname—Diz, which hardly seemed to fit him.
They talked about whether this year there shouldn't
be Chanukah lights as well as a crèche in the Center,

now that there were a fair number of Jews in town. They talked about ideas for new projects.

"May I say something?" she said.

"Sure," Frank Roddenberry and Herb Sundersen said. Coba was lying back in his chair looking at the ceiling (disparagingly, no doubt), his hands behind his head, his legs extended.

"Do you think there might be a chance of setting up some evening lectures for adults?" she asked. "Or parent-and-teenager forums? In one of the school auditoriums?"

"On what subject?" Frank Roddenberry asked.

"On any subject there's general interest in," she said. "The drug thing, which we're all concerned about but which the *Chronicle* seems to sweep under the rug; what rock music is all about—I don't know, *anything* that would get people out and listening and talking to each other."

"That's *interesting*," Claude Anselm-or-Axhelm said, leaning forward and crossing his legs, scratching at his temple. He was thin and blond; bright-eyed, restless.

"And maybe it would get the *women* out too," she said. "In case you don't know it, this town is a disaster area for baby-sitters."

Everyone laughed, and she felt good and at ease. She offered other possible forum topics, and Walter added a few, and so did Herb Sundersen. Other new-project ideas were brought up; she took part in the talk about them, and the men (except Coba, damn him) paid close attention to her—Ike Mazzard, Frank, Walter, Claude, even Herb looked right at her—and

they nodded and agreed with her, or thoughtfully
questioned her, and she felt very good indeed, meeting their questions with wit and good sense. *Move
over, Gloria Steinem!*

She saw, to her surprise and embarrassment, that
Ike Mazzard was sketching her. Sitting in his chair
(next to still-watching-the-ceiling Dale Coba), he was
pecking with a blue pen at a notebook on his dapper-
striped knee, looking at her and looking at his pecking.

Ike Mazzard! Sketching *her*!

The men had fallen silent. They looked into their
drinks, swirled their ice cubes.

"Hey," she said, shifting uncomfortably and smiling, "I'm no Ike Mazzard girl."

"Every girl's an Ike Mazzard girl," Mazzard said,
and smiled at her and smiled at his pecking.

She looked to Walter; he smiled embarrassedly and
shrugged.

She looked at Mazzard again, and—not moving her
head—at the other men. They looked at her and
smiled, edgily. "Well *this* is a conversation killer," she
said.

"Relax, you can move," Mazzard said. He turned a
page and pecked again.

Frank said, "I don't think another b-baseball field
is all that important."

She heard Kim cry "Mommy!" but Walter touched
her arm, and putting his glass down, got up and ex-
cused himself past Claude.

The men talked about new projects again. She said
a word or two, moving her head but aware all the

time of Mazzard looking at her and pecking. Try being Gloria Steinem when Ike Mazzard is drawing you! It was a bit show-offy of him; she wasn't any once-in-a-lifetime-mustn't-be-missed, not even in the Pucci loungers. And what were the *men* so tense about? Their talking seemed forced and gap-ridden. Herb Sundersen was actually blushing.

She felt suddenly as if she were naked, as if Mazzard were drawing her in obscene poses.

She crossed her legs; wanted to cross her arms too but didn't. *Jesus, Joanna, he's a show-offy artist, that's all. You're dressed.*

Walter came back and leaned down to her. "Just a bad dream," he said; and straightening, to the men, "Anyone want a refill? Diz? Frank?"

"I'll take a small one," Mazzard said, looking at her, pecking.

"Bathroom down that way?" Herb asked, getting up.

The talking went on, more relaxed and casual now.

New projects.

Old projects.

Mazzard tucked his pen into his jacket, smiling.

She said "Whew!" and fanned herself.

Coba raised his head, keeping his hands behind it, and chin-against-chest, looked at the notebook on Mazzard's knee. Mazzard turned pages, looking at Coba, and Coba nodded and said, "You never cease to amaze me."

"Do I get to see?" she asked.

"Of course!" Mazzard said, and half rose, smiling, holding out the open notebook to her.

Walter looked too, and Frank leaned in to see.

Portraits of her; there were page after page of them, small and precise—and flattering, as Ike Mazzard's work had always been. Full faces, three-quarter views, profiles; smiling, not smiling, talking, frowning.

"These are *beautiful*," Walter said, and Frank said, "Great, Ike!" Claude and Herb came around behind the sofa.

She leafed back through the pages. "They're—wonderful," she said. "I wish I could say they were absolutely accurate—"

"But they *are*!" Mazzard said.

"God bless you." She gave the notebook to him, and he put it on his knee and turned its pages, getting out his pen. He wrote on a page, and tore it out and offered it to her.

It was one of the three-quarter views, a non-smiling one, with the familiar no-capitals *ike mazzard* signature. She showed it to Walter; he said, "Thanks, Ike."

"My pleasure."

She smiled at Mazzard. "Thank you," she said. "I forgive you for blighting my adolescence." She smiled at all of them. "Does anyone want coffee?"

They all did, except Claude, who wanted tea.

She went into the kitchen and put the drawing on the place mats on top of the refrigerator. An Ike Mazzard drawing of *her*! Who'da thunk it, back home when she was eleven or twelve, reading Mom's *Jour-*

*nal*s and *Companion*s? It was foolish of her to have gotten so uptight about it. Mazzard had been nice to do it.

Smiling, she ran water into the coffee-maker, plugged it in, and put in the basket and spooned in coffee. She put the top on, pressed the plastic lid down onto the coffee can, and turned around. Coba leaned in the doorway watching her, his arms folded, his shoulder to the jamb.

Very cool in his jade turtleneck (matching his eyes, of course) and slate-gray corduroy suit.

He smiled at her and said, "I like to watch women doing little domestic chores."

"You came to the right town," she said. She tossed the spoon into the sink and took the coffee can to the refrigerator and put it in.

Coba stayed there, watching her.

She wished Walter would come. "You don't seem particularly dizzy," she said, getting out a saucepan for Claude's tea. "Why do they call you Diz?"

"I used to work at Disneyland," he said.

She laughed, going to the sink. "No, really," she said.

"That's really."

She turned around and looked at him.

"Don't you believe me?" he asked.

"No," she said.

"Why not?"

She thought, and knew.

"Why not?" he said. "Tell me."

To hell with him; she would. "You don't look like someone who enjoys making people happy."

Torpedoing forever, no doubt, the admission of women to the hallowed and sacrosanct Men's Association.

Coba looked at her—disparagingly. "How little you know," he said.

And smiled and got off the jamb, and turned and walked away.

"I'm not so keen on El Presidente," she said, undressing, and Walter said, "Neither am I. He's cold as ice. But he won't be in office forever."

"He'd better not be," she said, "or women'll never get in. When are elections?"

"Right after the first of the year."

"What does he do?"

"He's with Burnham-Massey, on Route Nine. So is Claude."

"Oh listen, what's his last name?"

"Claude's? Axhelm."

Kim began crying, and was burning hot; and they were up till after three, taking her temperature (a hundred and three at first), reading *Dr. Spock*, calling Dr. Verry, and giving her cool baths and alcohol rubs.

•　　　•　　　•

Bobbie found a live one. "At least she is compared to the rest of these clunks," her voice rasped from the phone. "Her name is Charmaine Wimperis, and if you squint a little she turns into Raquel Welch. They're up on Burgess Ridge in a two-hundred-thou-sand-dollar contemporary, and she's got a maid and a gardener and—now hear this—a tennis court."

"*Really?*"

"I thought that would get you out of the cellar. You're invited to play, and for lunch too. I'll pick you up around eleven-thirty."

"Today? I can't! Kim is still home."

"*Still?*"

"Could we make it Wednesday? Or Thursday, just to be safe."

"*Wednesday*," Bobbie said. "I'll check with her and call you back."

Wham! Pow! Slam! Charmaine was good, *too* god-damn good; the ball came zinging straight and hard, first to one side of the court and then to the other; it kept her racing from side to side and then drove her all the way back—a just-inside-the-liner that she barely caught. She ran in after it, but Charmaine smashed it down into the left net corner—ungettable—and took the game and the set, six-three. After tak-ing the first set six-two. "Oh God, I've had it!" Joanna said. "What a fiasco! *Oh boy!*"

"One more!" Charmaine called, backing to the serve line. "Come on, one more!"

"I can't! I'm not going to be able to walk tomorrow as it is!" She picked up the ball. "Come on, Bobbie, you play!"

Bobbie, sitting cross-legged on the grass outside the mesh fence, her face trayed on a sun reflector, said, "I haven't played since *camp*, for Chrissake."

"Just a game then!" Charmaine called. "One more game, Joanna!"

"All right, one more game!"

Charmaine won it.

"You killed me but it was great!" Joanna said as they walked off the court together. "Thank you!"

Charmaine, patting her high-boned cheeks carefully with an end of her towel, said, "You just have to get back in practice, that's all. You have a first-rate serve."

"Fat lot of good it did me."

"Will you play often? All I've got now are a couple of teen-age boys, both with permanent erections."

Bobbie said, "Send them to my place"—getting up from the ground.

They walked up the flagstone path toward the house.

"It's a terrific court," Joanna said, toweling her arm.

"Then *use* it," Charmaine said. "I used to play every day with Ginnie Fisher—do you know her?—but she flaked out on me. Don't *you*, will you? How about tomorrow?"

"Oh I couldn't!"

They sat on a terrace under a Cinzano umbrella, and the maid, a slight gray-haired woman named Nettie, brought them a pitcher of Bloody Marys and a bowl of cucumber dip and crackers. "She's marvelous," Charmaine said. "A German Virgo; if I told her to lick my shoes she'd do it. What are you, Joanna?"

"An American Taurus."

"If you tell her to lick your shoes she spits in your eye," Bobbie said. "You don't really believe that stuff, do you?"

"I certainly do," Charmaine said, pouring Bloody Marys. "You would too if you came to it with an open mind." (Joanna squinted at her: no, not Raquel Welch, but darn close.) "That's why Ginnie Fisher flaked out on me," she said. "She's a Gemini; they change all the time. Taureans are stable and dependable. Here's to tennis galore."

Joanna said, "This particular Taurean has a house and two kids and no German Virgo."

Charmaine had one child, a nine-year-old son named Merrill. Her husband Ed was a television producer. They had moved to Stepford in July. Yes, Ed was in the Men's Association, and no, Charmaine wasn't bothered by the sexist injustice. "Anything that gets him out of the house nights is fine with me," she said. "He's Aries and I'm Scorpio."

"Oh *well*," Bobbie said, and put a dip-loaded cracker into her mouth.

"It's a very bad combination," Charmaine said. "If I knew then what I know now."

"Bad in what way?" Joanna asked.

Which was a mistake. Charmaine told them at

length about her and Ed's manifold incompatibilities
—social, emotional, and above all, sexual. Nettie
served them lobster Newburg and julienne potatoes
—"Oi, my hips," Bobbie said, spooning lobster onto
her plate—and Charmaine went on in candid detail.
Ed was a sex fiend and a real weirdo. "He had this
rubber suit made for me, at God knows what cost, in
England. I ask you, *rubber?* 'Put it on one of your
secretaries,' I said, 'you're not going to get *me* into it.'
Zippers and padlocks all over. You can't lock up a
Scorpio. Virgos, any time; their thing is to serve. But
a Scorpio's thing is to go his own way."

"If *Ed* knew then what you know now," Joanna
said.

"It wouldn't have made the least bit of difference,"
Charmaine said. "He's crazy about me. Typical
Aries."

Nettie brought raspberry tarts and coffee. Bobbie
groaned. Charmaine told them about other weirdos
she had known. She had been a model and had known
several.

She walked them to Bobbie's car. "Now look," she
said to Joanna, "I know you're busy, but any time
you have a free hour, *any* time, just come on over. You
don't even have to call; I'm almost always here."

"Thanks, I will," Joanna said. "And thanks for today. It was great."

"*Any* time," Charmaine said. She leaned to the
window. "And look, both of you," she said, "would
you do me a favor? Would you read *Linda Goodman's
Sun Signs?* Just read it and see how right she is.

They've got it in the Center Pharmacy, in paper. Will
you? Please?"

They gave in, smiling, and promised they would.

"*Ciao!*" she called, waving to them as they drove
away.

"Well," Bobbie said, rounding the curve of the
driveway, "she may not be ideal NOW material, but
at least she's not in love with her vacuum cleaner."

"My God, she's beautiful," Joanna said.

"Isn't she? Even for these parts, where you've got
to admit they *look* good even if they don't think good.
Boy, what a marriage! How about that business with
the suit? And I thought *Dave* had spooky ideas!"

"Dave?" Joanna said, looking at her.

Bobbie side-flashed a smile. "You're not going to
get any true confessions out of *me*," she said. "I'm a
Leo, and our thing is changing the subject. You and
Walter want to go to a movie Saturday night?"

They had bought the house from a couple named Pil-
grim, who had lived in it for only two months and
had moved to Canada. The Pilgrims had bought it
from a Mrs. McGrath, who had bought it from the
builder eleven years before. So most of the junk in
the storage room had been left by Mrs. McGrath. Actually it wasn't fair to call it junk: there were two
good Colonial side chairs that Walter was going to
strip and refinish someday; there was a complete
twenty-volume *Book of Knowledge,* now on the shelves

in Pete's room; and there were boxes and small bundles of hardware and oddments that, though not finds, at least seemed likely to be of eventual use. Mrs. McGrath had been a thoughtful saver.

Joanna had transferred most of the not-really-junk to a far corner of the cellar before the plumber had installed the sink, and now she was moving the last of it—cans of paint and bundles of asbestos roof shingles —while Walter hammered at a plywood counter and Pete handed him nails. Kim had gone with the Van Sant girls and Carol to the library.

Joanna unrolled a packet of yellowed newspaper and found inside it an inch-wide paintbrush, its clean bristles slightly stiff but still pliable. She began rolling it back into the paper, a half page of the *Chronicle*, and the words *WOMEN'S CLUB* caught her eye. *HEARS AUTHOR.* She turned the paper to the side and looked at it.

"For God's sake," she said.

Pete looked at her, and Walter, hammering, said, "What is it?"

She got the brush out of the paper and put it down, and held the half page open with both hands, reading.

Walter stopped hammering and turned and looked at her. "What is it?" he asked.

She read for another moment, and looked at him; and looked at the paper, and at him. "There was—a *women's* club here," she said. "Betty Friedan spoke to them. And *Kit Sundersen* was the president. Dale Coba's wife and Frank Roddenberry's wife were officers."

"Are you kidding?" he said.

She looked at the paper, and read: " 'Betty Friedan, the author of *The Feminine Mystique*, addressed members of the Stepford Women's Club Tuesday evening in the Fairview Lane home of Mrs. Herbert Sundersen, the club's president. Over fifty women applauded Mrs. Friedan as she cited the inequities and frustrations besetting the modern-day housewife . . .' " She looked at him.

"Can I do some?" Pete asked.

Walter handed the hammer to him. "When *was* that?" he asked her.

She looked at the paper. "It doesn't say, it's the bottom half," she said. "There's a picture of the officers. 'Mrs. Steven Margolies, Mrs. Dale Coba, author Betty Friedan, Mrs. Herbert Sundersen, Mrs. Frank Roddenberry, and Mrs. Duane T. Anderson.' " She opened the half page toward him, and he came to her and took a side of it. "If this doesn't beat everything," he said, looking at the picture and the article.

"I *spoke* to Kit Sundersen," she said. "She didn't say a *word* about it. She didn't have time for a get-together. Like all the others."

"This must have been six or seven years ago," he said, fingering the edge of the yellowed paper.

"Or more," she said. "The *Mystique* came out while I was still working. Andreas gave me his review copy, remember?"

He nodded, and turned to Pete, who was hammering vigorously at the counter top. "Hey, take it easy," he said, "you'll make half moons." He turned back to the paper. "Isn't this something?" he said. "It must have just petered out."

"With fifty members?" she said. "*Over* fifty? Applauding Friedan, not hissing her?"

"Well it's not here now, is it?" he said, letting the paper go. "Unless they've got the world's worst publicity chairman. I'll ask Herb what happened next time I see him." He went back to Pete. "Say, that's good work," he said.

She looked at the paper and shook her head. "I can't believe it," she said. "Who were the women? They can't all have moved away."

"Come on now," Walter said, "you haven't spoken to every woman in town."

"Bobbie has, darn near," she said. She folded the paper, and folded it, and put it on the carton of her equipment. The paintbrush was there; she picked it up. "Need a paintbrush?" she said.

Walter turned and looked at her. "You don't expect me to *paint* these things, do you?" he asked.

"No, no," she said. "It was wrapped in the paper."

"Oh," he said, and turned to the counter.

She put the brush down, and crouched and gathered a few loose shingles. "How could she not have mentioned it?" she said. "She was the *president*."

As soon as Bobbie and Dave got into the car, she told them.

"Are you sure it's not one of those newspapers

they print in penny arcades?" Bobbie said. "'Fred Smith Lays Elizabeth Taylor'?"

"It's the *Chronic Ill*," Joanna said. "The bottom half of the front page. Here, if you can see."

She handed it back to them, and they unfolded it between them. Walter turned on the top light.

Dave said, "You could have made a lot of money by betting me and *then* showing me."

"Didn't think," she said.

"'Over fifty women'!" Bobbie said. "Who the hell were they? What happened?"

"That's what *I* want to know," she said. "And why Kit Sundersen didn't mention it to me. I'm going to speak to her tomorrow."

They drove into Eastbridge and stood on line for the nine o'clock showing of an R-rated English movie. The couples in the line were cheerful and talkative, laughing in clusters of four and six, looking to the end of the line, waving at other couples. None of them looked familiar except an elderly couple Bobbie recognized from the Historical Society; and the seventeen-year-old McCormick boy and a date, holding hands solemnly, trying to look eighteen.

The movie, they agreed, was "bloody good," and after it they drove back to Bobbie and Dave's house, which was chaotic, the boys still up and the sheepdog galumphing all over. When Bobbie and Dave had got rid of the sitter and the boys and the sheepdog, they had coffee and cheesecake in the tornado-struck living room.

"I *knew* I wasn't uniquely irresistible," Joanna said,

looking at an Ike Mazzard drawing of Bobbie tucked in the frame of the over-the-mantel picture.

"Every girl's an Ike Mazzard girl, didn't you know?" Bobbie said, tucking the drawing more securely into the frame's corner, making the picture more crooked than it already was. "Boy, I wish I looked *half* this good."

"You're fine the way you are," Dave said, standing behind them.

"Isn't he a doll?" Bobbie said to Joanna. She turned and kissed Dave's cheek. "It's *still* your Sunday to get up early," she said.

"Joanna Eberhart," Kit Sundersen said, and smiled. "How are you? Would you like to come in?"

"Yes, I would," Joanna said, "if you have a few minutes."

"Of course I do, come on in," Kit said. She was a pretty woman, black-haired and dimple-cheeked, and only slightly older-looking than in the *Chronicle's* unflattering photo. About thirty-three, Joanna guessed, going into the entrance hall. Its ivory vinyl floor looked as if one of those plastic shields in the commercials had just floated down onto it. Sounds of a baseball game came from the living room.

"Herb is inside with Gary Claybrook," Kit said, closing the front door. "Do you want to say hello to them?"

Joanna went to the living-room archway and

looked in: Herb and Gary were sitting on a sofa
watching a large color TV across the room. Gary was
holding half a sandwich and chewing. A plate of
sandwiches and two cans of beer stood on a cobbler's
bench before them. The room was beige and brown
and green; Colonial, immaculate. Joanna waited till a
retreating ballplayer caught the ball, and said, "Hi."

Herb and Gary turned and smiled. "Hello,
Joanna," they said, and Gary said, "How are you?"
Herb said, "Is Walter here too?"

"Fine. No, he isn't," she said. "I just came over to
talk with Kit. Good game?"

Herb looked away from her, and Gary said,
"Very."

Kit, beside her and smelling of Walter's mother's
perfume, whatever it was, said, "Come, let's go into
the kitchen."

"Enjoy," she said to Herb and Gary. Gary, biting
into his sandwich, eye-smiled through his glasses, and
Herb looked at her and said, "Thanks, we will."

She followed Kit over the plastic-shield vinyl.

"Would you like a cup of coffee?" Kit asked.

"No, thanks." She followed Kit into the coffee-
smelling kitchen. It was immaculate, of course—except for the open dryer, and the clothes and the laundry basket on the counter on top of it. The washer's
round port was storming. The floor was more plastic
shield.

"It's right on the stove," Kit said, "so it wouldn't
be any trouble."

"Well in that case . . ."

She sat at a round green table while Kit got a cup

and saucer from a neatly filled cabinet, the cups all hook-hung, the plates filed in racks. "It's nice and quiet now," Kit said, closing the cabinet and going toward the stove. (Her figure, in a short sky-blue dress, was almost as terrific as Charmaine's.) "The kids are over at Gary and Donna's," she said. "I'm doing Marge McCormick's wash. She's got a bug of some kind and can barely move today."

"Oh that's a shame," Joanna said.

Kit fingertipped the top of a percolator and poured coffee from it. "I'm sure she'll be good as new in a day or two," she said. "How do you take this, Joanna?"

"Milk, no sugar, please."

Kit carried the cup and saucer toward the refrigerator. "If it's about that get-together again," she said, "I'm afraid I'm still awfully busy."

"It isn't that," Joanna said. She watched Kit open the refrigerator. "I wanted to find out what happened to the Women's Club," she said.

Kit stood at the lighted refrigerator, her back to Joanna. "The Women's Club?" she said. "Oh my, that was years ago. It disbanded."

"Why?" Joanna asked.

Kit closed the refrigerator and opened a drawer beside it. "Some of the women moved away," she said —she closed the drawer and turned, putting a spoon on the saucer—"and the rest of us just lost interest in it. At least I did." She came toward the table, watching the cup. "It wasn't accomplishing anything useful," she said. "The meetings got boring after a while." She put the cup and saucer on the table and pushed them closer to Joanna. "Is that enough milk?" she asked.

"Yes, that's fine," Joanna said. "Thanks. How come you didn't tell me about it when I was here the other time?"

Kit smiled, her dimples deepening. "You didn't ask me," she said. "If you had I would have told you. It's no secret. Would you like a piece of cake, or some cookies?"

"No, thanks," Joanna said.

"I'm going to fold these things," Kit said, going from the table.

Joanna watched her close the dryer and take something white from the pile of clothes on it. She shook it out—a T-shirt. Joanna said, "What's wrong with *Bill* McCormick? Can't *he* run a washer? I thought he was one of our aerospace brains."

"He's taking care of Marge," Kit said, folding the T-shirt. "These things came out nice and white, didn't they?" She put the folded T-shirt into the laundry basket, smiling.

Like an actress in a commercial.

That's what she was, Joanna felt suddenly. That's what they *all* were, all the Stepford wives: actresses in commercials, pleased with detergents and floor wax, with cleansers, shampoos, and deodorants. Pretty actresses, big in the bosom but small in the talent, playing suburban housewives unconvincingly, too nicey-nice to be real.

"Kit," she said.

Kit looked at her.

"You must have been very young when you were

president of the club," Joanna said. "Which means you're intelligent and have a certain amount of drive. Are you happy now? Tell me the truth. Do you feel you're living a full life?"

Kit looked at her, and nodded. "Yes, I'm happy," she said. "I feel I'm living a very full life. Herb's work is important, and he couldn't do it nearly as well if not for me. We're a unit, and between us we're raising a family, and doing optical research, and running a clean comfortable household, and doing community work."

"Through the Men's Association."

"Yes."

Joanna said, "Were the Women's Club meetings more boring than housework?"

Kit frowned. "No," she said, "but they weren't as useful as housework. You're not drinking your coffee. Is anything wrong with it?"

"No," Joanna said, "I was waiting for it to cool." She picked up the cup.

"Oh," Kit said, and smiled, and turned to the clothes and folded something.

Joanna watched her. Should she ask who the other women had been? No, they would be like Kit; and what difference would it make? She drank from the cup. The coffee was strong and rich-flavored, the best she'd tasted in a long time.

"How are your children?" Kit asked.

"Fine," she said.

She started to ask the brand of the coffee, but stopped herself and drank more of it.

•   •   •

Maybe the hardware store's panes would have wobbled the moon's reflection interestingly, but there was no way of telling, not with the panes where *they* were and the moon where *it* was. *C'est la vie.* She mooched around the Center for a while, getting the feel of the night-empty curve of street, the row of white shopfronts on one side, the rise to the hill on the other; the library, the Historical Society cottage. She wasted some film on streetlights and litter baskets—cliché time—but it was only black-and-white, so what the hell. A cat trotted down the path from the library, a silver-gray cat with a black moonshadow stuck to its paws; it crossed the street toward the market parking lot. No, thanks, we're not keen on cat pix.

She set up the tripod on the library lawn and took shots of the shopfronts, using the fifty-millimeter lens and making ten-, twelve-, and fourteen-second exposures. An odd medicinal smell soured the air—coming on the breeze at her back. It almost reminded her of something in her childhood, but fell short. A syrup she'd been given? A toy she had had?

She reloaded by moonlight, gathered the tripod, and backed across the street, scouting the library for a good angle. She found one and set up. The white clapboard siding was black-banded in the overhead moonlight; the windows showed bookshelved walls lighted faintly from within. She focused with extra-special care, and starting at eight seconds, took each-a-second-longer exposures up to eighteen. One of them, at least, would catch the inside bookshelved walls without overexposing the siding.

She went to the car for her sweater, and looked around as she went back to the camera. The Historical Society cottage? No, it was too tree-shadowed, and dull anyway. But the Men's Association house, up on the hill, had a surprisingly comic look to it: a square old nineteenth-century house, solid and symmetrical, tipsily parasolled by a glistening TV antenna. The four tall upstairs windows were vividly alight, their sashes raised. Figures moved inside.

She took the fifty-millimeter lens out of the camera and was putting in the one-thirty-five when headlight beams swept onto the street and grew brighter. She turned and a spotlight blinded her. Closing her eyes, she tightened the lens; then shielded her eyes and squinted.

The car stopped, and the spotlight swung away and died to an orange spark. She blinked a few times, still seeing the blinding radiance.

A police car. It stayed where it was, about thirty feet away from her on the other side of the street. A man's voice spoke softly inside it; spoke and kept speaking.

She waited.

The car moved forward, coming opposite her, and stopped. The young policeman with the un-policeman-like brown mustache smiled at her and said, "Evening, ma'am." She had seen him several times, once in the stationery store buying packs of colored crepe paper, one each of every color they had.

"Hello," she said, smiling.

He was alone in the car; he must have been talking on his radio. About her? "I'm sorry I hit you with the spot that way," he said. "Is that your car there by the post office?"

"Yes," she said. "I didn't park it here because I was—"

"That's all right, I'm just checking." He squinted at the camera. "That's a good-looking camera," he said. "What kind is it?"

"A Pentax," she said.

"Pentax," he said. He looked at the camera, and at her. "And you can take pictures at night with it?"

"Time exposures," she said.

"Oh, sure," he said. "How long does it take, on a night like this?"

"Well that depends," she said.

He wanted to know on what, and what kind of film she was using. And whether she was a professional photographer, and how much a Pentax cost, just roughly. And how it stacked up against other cameras.

She tried not to grow impatient; she should be glad she lived in a town where a policeman could stop and talk for a few minutes.

Finally he smiled and said, "Well, I guess I'd better let you go ahead with it. Good night."

"Good night," she said, smiling.

He drove off slowly. The silver-gray cat ran through his headlight beams.

She watched the car for a moment, and then turned to the camera and checked the lens. Crouching to the viewfinder, she levered into a good framing of the Men's Association house and locked the tripod head. She focused, sharpening the finder's image of the high square tipsy-antennaed house. Two of its upstairs windows were dark now; and another was shade-pulled down to darkness, and then the last one.

She straightened and looked at the house itself, and turned to the police car's faraway taillights.

He had radioed a message about her, and then he had stalled her with his questions while the message was acted on, the shades pulled down.

Oh come on, girl, you're getting nutty! She looked at the house again. They wouldn't have a *radio* up there. And what would he have been afraid she'd photograph? An orgy in progress? Call girls from the city? (Or better yet, from right there in Stepford.) *EN-LARGER REVEALS SHOCKING SECRET. Seemingly diligent housewives, conveniently holding still for lengthy time exposures, were caught Sunday night disporting at the Men's Association house by photographer Nancy Drew Eber-hart of Fairview Lane . . .*

Smiling, she crouched to the viewfinder, bettered her framing and focus, and took three shots of the dark-windowed house—ten seconds, twelve, and fourteen.

She took shots of the post office, and of its bare flagpole silhouetted against moonlit clouds.

She was putting the tripod into the car when the police car came by and slowed. "Hope they all come out!" the young policeman called.

"Thanks!" she called back to him. "I enjoyed talking!" To make up for her city-bred suspiciousness.

"Good night!" the policeman called.

A senior partner in Walter's firm died of uremic poisoning, and the records of the trusts he had administered were found to be disquietingly inaccurate. Walter had to stay two nights and a weekend in the city, and on the nights following he seldom got home before eleven o'clock. Pete took a fall on the school bus and knocked out his two front teeth. Joanna's parents paid a short-notice three-day visit on their way to a Caribbean vacation. (They loved the house and Stepford, and Joanna's mother admired Carol Van Sant. "So serene and efficient! Take a leaf from *her* book, Joanna.")

The dishwasher broke down, and the pump; and Pete's eighth birthday came, calling for presents, a party, favors, a cake. Kim got a sore throat and was home for three days. Joanna's period was late but came, thank God and the Pill.

She managed to get in a little tennis, her game improving but still not as good as Charmaine's. She got the darkroom three-quarters set up and made trial enlargements of the black-man-and-taxi picture, and developed and printed the ones she had taken in the Center, two of which looked very good. She took shots of Pete and Kim and Scott Chamalian playing on the jungle gym.

She saw Bobbie almost every day; they shopped together, and sometimes Bobbie brought her two younger boys Adam and Kenny over after school. One day Joanna and Bobbie and Charmaine got dressed to the nines and had a two-cocktail lunch at a French restaurant in Eastbridge.

By the end of October, Walter was getting home for dinner again, the dead partner's peculations having been unraveled, made good, and patched over. Everything in the house was working, everyone was well. They carved a huge pumpkin for Halloween, and Pete went trick-or-treating as a front-toothless Batman, and Kim as Heckel or Jeckel (she was both, she insisted). Joanna gave out fifty bags of candy and had to fall back on fruit and cookies; next year she would know better.

On the first Saturday in November they gave a dinner party: Bobbie and Dave, Charmaine and her husband Ed; and from the city, Shep and Sylvia Tackover, and Don Ferrault—one of Walter's partners—and his wife Lucy. The local woman Joanna got to help serve and clean up was delighted to be working in Stepford for a change. "There used to be *so* much entertaining here!" she said. "I had a whole *round* of women that used to *fight* over me! And now I have to go to *Nor*wood, and *East*bridge, and New *Shar*on! And I *hate* night driving!" She was a plump quick-moving white-haired woman named Mary Migliardi. "It's that Men's Association," she said, jabbing toothpicks into shrimp on a platter. "Entertaining's gone right out the window since *they* started up!

The men go out and the women stay in! If my old man was alive he'd have to knock me on the head before I'd let him join!"

"But it's a very old organization, isn't it?" Joanna said, tossing salad at arm's length because of her dress.

"Are you kidding?" Mary said. "It's new! Six or seven years, that's all. Before, there was the Civic Association and the Elks and the Legion"—she toothpicked shrimp with machinelike rapidity—"but they all merged in with it once it got going. Except the Legion; they're still separate. Six or seven years, that's all. This isn't all you got for hors d'oeuvres, is it?"

"There's a cheese roll in the refrigerator," Joanna said.

Walter came in, looking very handsome in his plaid jacket, carrying the ice bucket. "We're in luck," he said, going to the refrigerator. "There's a good Creature Feature; Pete doesn't even want to come down. I put the Sony in his room." He opened the freezer section and took out a bag of ice cubes.

"Mary just told me the Men's Association is new," Joanna said.

"It's not *new*," Walter said, tearing at the top of the bag. A white dab of tissue clung to his jawbone, pinned by a dot of dried blood.

"Six or seven years," Mary said.

"Where we come from that's old."

Joanna said, "I thought it went back to the Puritans."

"What gave you that idea?" Walter asked, spilling ice cubes into the bucket.

She tossed the salad. "I don't know," she said. "The way it's set up, and that old house . . ."

"That was the Terhune place," Mary said, laying a stretch of plastic over the toothpicked platter. "They got it dirt-cheap. Auctioned for taxes and no one else bid."

The party was a disaster. Lucy Ferrault was allergic to something and never stopped sneezing; Sylvia was preoccupied; Bobbie, whom Joanna had counted on as a conversational star, had laryngitis. Charmaine was Miss Vamp, provocative and come-hithery in floor-length white silk cut clear to her navel; Dave and Shep were provoked and went thither. Walter (*damn* him!) talked law in the corner with Don Ferrault. Ed Wimperis—big, fleshy, well tailored, stewed —talked television, clamping Joanna's arm and explaining in slow careful words why cassettes were going to change everything. At the dinner table Sylvia got unpreoccupied and tore into suburban communities that enriched themselves with tax-yielding light industry while fortressing themselves with two- and four-acre zoning. Ed Wimperis knocked his wine over. Joanna tried to get light conversation going, and Bobbie pitched in valiantly, gasping an explanation of where the laryngitis had come from: she was doing tape-recordings for a friend of Dave's who "thinks 'e's a bleedin' 'Enry 'Iggins, 'e does." But Charmaine, who knew the man and had taped for him herself, cut her short with "Never make fun of what a Capricorn's doing; they *produce*," and went into an around-the-table sign analysis that demanded everyone's attention. The roast was overdone, and Walter had a bad time slicing it. The soufflé rose, but not quite as much as it should have—as Mary remarked while serving it. Lucy Ferrault sneezed.

"Never again," Joanna said as she switched the outside lights off; and Walter, yawning, said, "Soon enough for me."

"Listen, you," she said. "How could you stand there talking to Don while three women are sitting like stones on the sofa?"

Sylvia called to apologize—she had been passed up for a promotion she damn well knew she deserved—and Charmaine called to say they'd had a great time and to postpone a tentative Tuesday tennis date. "Ed's got a bee in his bonnet," she said. "He's taking a few days off, we're putting Merrill with the DaCostas—you don't know them, lucky you—and he and I are going to 'rediscover each other.' That means he chases me around the bed. And my period's not till next week, God damn it."

"Why not let him catch you?" Joanna said.

"Oh God," Charmaine said. "Look, I just don't enjoy having a big cock shoved into me, that's all. Never have and never will. And I'm not a lez either, because I tried it and *that's* no big deal. I'm just not interested in sex. I don't think any woman is, really, not even Pisces women. Are you?"

"Well I'm not a nympho," Joanna said, "but I'm interested in it, sure I am."

"*Really*, or do you just feel you're supposed to be?"

"Really."

"Well, to each his own," Charmaine said. "Let's make it Thursday, all right? He's got a conference he can't get out of, thank God."

"Okay, Thursday, unless something comes up."

"Don't *let* anything."

"It's getting cold."

"We'll wear sweaters."

She went to a P.T.A. meeting. Pete's and Kim's teachers were there, Miss Turner and Miss Gair, pleasant middle-aged women eagerly responsive to her questions about teaching methods and how the busing program was working out. The meeting was poorly attended; aside from the group of teachers at the back of the auditorium, there were only nine women and about a dozen men. The president of the association was an attractive blond woman named Mrs. Hollingsworth, who conducted business with smiling unhurried efficiency.

She bought winter clothes for Pete and Kim, and two pairs of wool slacks for herself. She made terrific enlargements of "Off Duty" and "The Stepford Library," and took Pete and Kim to Dr. Coe, the dentist.

.   .   .

"Did we?" Charmaine asked, letting her into the house.

"Of course we did," she said. "I said it was okay if nothing came up."

Charmaine closed the door and smiled at her. She was wearing an apron over slacks and a blouse. "Gosh, I'm sorry, Joanna," she said. "I completely forgot."

"That's all right," she said, "go change."

"We can't play," Charmaine said. "For one thing, I've got too much work to do—"

"Work?"

"Housework."

Joanna looked at her.

"We've let Nettie go," Charmaine said. "It's absolutely unbelievable, the sloppy job she was getting away with. The place looks clean at first glance, but boy, look in the corners. I did the kitchen and the dining room yesterday, but I've still got all the other rooms. Ed shouldn't have to live with dirt."

Joanna, looking at her, said, "Okay, funny joke."

"I'm not joking," Charmaine said. "Ed's a pretty wonderful guy, and I've been lazy and selfish. I'm through playing tennis, and I'm through reading those astrology books. From now on I'm going to do right by Ed, and by Merrill too. I'm lucky to have such a wonderful husband and son."

Joanna looked at the pressed and covered racket in

her hand, and at Charmaine. "That's great," she said, and smiled. "But I honestly can't believe you're giving up tennis."

"Go look," Charmaine said.

Joanna looked at her.

"Go look," Charmaine said.

Joanna turned and went into the living room and across it to the glass doors. She slid one open, hearing Charmaine behind her, and went out onto the terrace. She crossed the terrace and looked down the slope of flagstone-pathed lawn.

A truck piled with sections of mesh fencing stood on the tire-marked grass beside the tennis court. Two sides of the court's fence were gone, and the other two lay flat on the grass, a long side and a short one. Two men kneeled on the long side, working at it with long-handled cutters. They brought the handles up and together, and clicks of sound followed. A mountain of dark soil sat on the center of the court; the net and the posts were gone.

"Ed wants a putting green," Charmaine said, coming to Joanna's side.

"It's a *clay court*!" Joanna said, turning to her.

"It's the only level place we've got," Charmaine said.

"My God," Joanna said, looking at the men working the cutter handles. "That's crazy, Charmaine!"

"Ed plays golf, he doesn't play tennis," Charmaine said.

Joanna looked at her. "What did he *do* to you?" she said. "*Hypnotize* you?"

"Don't be silly," Charmaine said, smiling. "He's a

wonderful guy and I'm a lucky woman who ought to
be grateful to him. Do you want to stay awhile? I'll
make you some coffee. I'm doing Merrill's room but
we can talk while I'm working."

"All right," Joanna said, but shook her head and
said, "No, no, I—" She backed from Charmaine, looking at her. "No, there are things *I* should be doing
too." She turned and went quickly across the terrace.

"I'm sorry I forgot to call you," Charmaine said,
following her into the living room.

"It's all right," Joanna said, going quickly, stopping, turning, holding her racket before her with
both hands. "I'll see you in a few days, okay?"

"Yes," Charmaine said, smiling. "Please call me.
And please give my regards to Walter."

Bobbie went to see for herself, and called about it.
"She was moving the bedroom furniture. And they
just moved in in July; how dirty can the place be?"

"It won't last," Joanna said. "It can't. People don't
change that way."

"Don't they?" Bobbie said. "Around here?"

"What do you mean?"

"Shut up, Kenny! Give him that! Joanna, listen, I
want to talk with you. Can you have lunch tomorrow?"

"Yes—"

"I'll pick you up around noon. I said *give* it to him!
Okay? Noon, nothing fancy."

"Okay. Kim! You're getting water all over the—"

Walter wasn't particularly surprised to hear about the change in Charmaine. "Ed must have laid the law down to her," he said, turning a fork of spaghetti against his spoon. "I don't think he makes enough money for that kind of a setup. A maid must be at *least* a hundred a week these days."

"But her whole *attitude's* changed," Joanna said. "You'd think she'd be complaining."

"Do you know what Jeremy's allowance is?" Pete said.

"He's two years older than you are," Walter said.

"This is going to sound crazy, but I want you to listen to me without laughing, because either I'm right or I'm going off my rocker and need sympathy." Bobbie picked at the bun of her cheeseburger.

Joanna, watching her, swallowed cheeseburger and said, "All right, go ahead."

They were at the McDonald's on Eastbridge Road, eating in the car.

Bobbie took a small bite of her cheeseburger, and chewed and swallowed. "There was a thing in *Time* a few weeks ago," she said. "I looked for it but I must have thrown the issue out." She looked at Joanna. "They have a very low crime rate in El Paso, Texas," she said. "I *think* it was El Paso. Anyway, *somewhere* in Texas they have a very low crime rate, much lower than anywhere *else* in Texas; and the reason is, there's a chemical in the ground that gets into the water, and it tranquilizes everybody and eases the tension. God's truth."

"I think I remember," Joanna said, nodding, holding her cheeseburger.

"Joanna," Bobbie said, "I think there's something *here*. In Stepford. It's possible, isn't it? All those fancy plants on Route Nine—electronics, computers, aerospace junk, with Stepford Creek running right behind them—who knows *what* kind of crap they're dumping into the environment."

"What do you *mean?*" Joanna said.

"Just think for a minute," Bobbie said. She fisted her free hand and stuck out its pinky. "Charmaine's changed and become a hausfrau," she said. She stuck out her ring finger. "The woman you spoke to, the one who was president of the club; *she* changed, didn't she, from what she must have been before?"

Joanna nodded.

Bobbie's next finger flicked out. "The woman Charmaine played tennis with, before you; she changed too, Charmaine said so."

Joanna frowned. She took a French fry from the bag between them. "You think it's—because of a *chemical?*" she said.

Bobbie nodded. "Either leaking from one of those plants, or just *around*, like in El Paso or wherever." She took her coffee from the dashboard. "It *has* to be," she said. "It can't be a coincidence that Stepford women are all the way they are. And some of the ones we spoke to *must* have belonged to that club. A few years ago they were *applauding Betty Friedan*, and look at them now. *They've changed too.*"

Joanna ate the French fry and took a bite of her cheeseburger. Bobbie took a bite of her cheeseburger and sipped her coffee.

"There's *something*," Bobbie said. "In the ground, in the water, in the air—I don't know. It makes women interested in housekeeping and nothing else but. Who knows what chemicals can do? *Nobel-prize winners* don't even really know yet. Maybe it's some kind of hormone thing; that would explain the fantastic boobs. You've got to have noticed."

"I sure have," Joanna said. "I feel pre-adolescent every time I set foot in the market."

"*I* do, for God's sake," Bobbie said. She put her coffee on the dashboard and took French fries from the bag. "Well?" she said.

"I suppose it's—possible," Joanna said. "But it sounds so—fantastic." She took her coffee from the dashboard; it had made a patch of fog on the windshield.

"No more fantastic than El Paso," Bobbie said.

"More," Joanna said. "Because it affects only women. What does Dave think?"

"I haven't mentioned it to him yet. I thought I'd try it out on you first."

Joanna sipped her coffee. "Well it's in the realm of *possibility*," she said. "I *don't* think you're off your rocker. The thing to do, I guess, is write a very level-headed-sounding letter to the State—what, Department of Health? Environmental Commission?

Whatever agency would have the authority to look into it. We could find out at the library."

Bobbie shook her head. "Mm-mmn," she said. "I *worked* for a government agency; forget it. *I* think the thing to do is move out. *Then* futz around with letters."

Joanna looked at her.

"I mean it," Bobbie said. "Anything that can make a hausfrau out of *Charmaine* isn't going to have any special trouble with *me*. *Or* with *you*."

"Oh come *on*," Joanna said.

"There's something here, Joanna! I'm not kidding! This is Zombieville! And Charmaine moved in in July, *I* moved in in August, and *you* moved in in September!"

"All right, quiet down, I can hear."

Bobbie took a large-mouthed bite of her cheeseburger. Joanna sipped her coffee and frowned.

"Even if I'm wrong," Bobbie said with her mouth full, "even if there's no chemical doing anything"— she swallowed—"is this where you really want to live? We've each got one friend now, you after two months, me after three. Is *that* your idea of the ideal community? I went into Norwood to get my hair done for your party; I saw a *dozen* women who were rushed and sloppy and irritated and alive; I wanted to hug every one of them!"

"Find friends in Norwood," Joanna said, smiling. "You've got the car."

"You're so damn independent!" Bobbie took her coffee from the dashboard. "I'm asking Dave to move," she said. "We'll sell here and buy in Norwood or Eastbridge; all it'll mean is some headaches and bother and the moving costs—for which, if he insists, I'll hock the rock."

"Do you think he'll agree?"

"He damn well better had, or his life is going to get mighty miserable. I wanted to buy in Norwood all along; too many WASPs, he said. Well I'd rather get stung by WASPs than poisoned by whatever's working around here. So you're going to be down to no friends at all in a little while—unless *you* speak to *Walter*."

"About *moving?*"

Bobbie nodded. Looking at Joanna, she sipped her coffee.

Joanna shook her head. "I couldn't ask him to move again," she said.

"Why not? He wants you to be happy, doesn't he?"

"I'm not sure that I'm not. And I just finished the darkroom."

"Okay," Bobbie said, "stick around. Turn into your next-door neighbor."

"Bobbie, it *can't* be a chemical. I mean it *could*, but I honestly don't believe it. Honestly."

They talked about it while they finished eating, and then they drove up Eastbridge Road and turned onto Route Nine. They passed the shopping mall and the antique stores, and came to the industrial plants.

"Poisoner's Row," Bobbie said.

Joanna looked at the neat low modern buildings, set back from the road and separated each from the next by wide spans of green lawn: Ulitz Optics (where Herb Sundersen worked), and CompuTech

(Vic Stavros, or was he with Instatron?), and Steven-son Biochemical, and Haig-Darling Computers, and Burnham-Massey-Microtech (Dale Coba—hiss!—and Claude Axhelm), and Instatron, and Reed & Saunders (Bill McCormick—how was Marge?), and Vesey Electronics, and AmeriChem Willis.

"Nerve-gas research, I'll bet you five bucks."

"In a *populated area*?"

"Why not? With that gang in Washington?"

"Oh come *on*, Bobbie!"

Walter saw something was bothering her and asked her about it. She said, "You've got the Koblenz agreement to do," but he said, "I've got all weekend. Come on, what is it?"

So while she scraped the dishes and put them in the washer, she told him about Bobbie's wanting to move, and her "El Paso" theory.

"That sounds pretty far-fetched to me," he said.

"To me too," she said. "But women *do* seem to change around here, and what they change into is pretty damn dull. If Bobbie moves, and if Charmaine doesn't come back to her old self, which at least was—"

"Do *you* want to move?" he asked.

She looked uncertainly at him. His blue eyes, waiting for her answer, gave no clue to his feelings. "No," she said, "not when we're all settled in. It's a good house . . . And yes, I'm sure I'd be happier in Eastbridge or Norwood. I wish we'd looked in either one of them."

"*There's* an unequivocal answer," he said, smiling. " 'No and yes.' "

"About sixty-forty," she said.

He straightened from the counter he had been leaning against. "All right," he said, "if it gets to be zero–a hundred, we'll do it."

"You would?" she said.

"Sure," he said, "if you were really unhappy. I wouldn't want to do it during the school year—"

"No, no, of course not."

"But we could do it next summer. I don't think we'd lose anything, except the time and the moving and closing costs."

"That's what Bobbie said."

"So it's just a matter of making up your mind." He looked at his watch and went out of the kitchen.

"Walter?" she called, touching her hands to a towel.

"Yes?"

She went to where she could see him, standing in the hallway. "Thanks," she said, smiling. "I feel better."

"You're the one who has to be here all day, not me," he said, and smiled at her and went into the den.

She watched him go, then turned and glanced through the port to the family room. Pete and Kim sat on the floor watching TV—President Kennedy and President Johnson, surprisingly; no, figures of them. She watched for a moment, and went back to the sink and scraped the last few dishes.

.   .   .

Dave, too, was willing to move at the end of the
school year. "He gave in so easily I thought I'd keel
over," Bobbie said on the phone the next morning. "I
just hope we *make* it till June."

"Drink bottled water," Joanna said.

"You think I'm not going to? I just sent Dave to get
some."

Joanna laughed.

"Go ahead, laugh," Bobbie said. "For a few cents a
day I'd rather be safe than sorry. And I'm writing to
the Department of Health. The problem is, how do I
do it without coming across like a little old lady without all her marbles? You want to help, and co-sign?"

"Sure," Joanna said. "Come on over later. Walter is
drafting a trust agreement; maybe he'll lend us a few
whereases."

She made autumn-leaf collages with Pete and Kim,
and helped Walter put up the storm windows, and
met him in the city for a partners-and-wives dinner—
the usual falsely-friendly clothes-appraising bore. A
check came from the agency: two hundred dollars for
four uses of her best picture.

She met Marge McCormick in the market—yes,
she'd had a bug but now she was fine, thanks—and

Frank Roddenberry in the hardware store—"Hello, Joanna, how've you b-been?"—and the Welcome Wagon lady right outside. "A black family is moving in on Gwendolyn Lane. But I think it's *good*, don't you?"

"Yes, I do."

"All ready for winter?"

"I am now." Smiling, she showed the sack of birdseed she'd just bought.

"It's beautiful here!" the Welcome Wagon lady said. "You're the shutterbug, aren't you? You should have a field day!"

She called Charmaine and invited her for lunch. "I can't, Joanna, I'm sorry," Charmaine said. "I've got so much to do around the house here. You know how it is."

Claude Axhelm came over one Saturday afternoon— to see her, not Walter. He had a briefcase with him.

"I've got this project I've been working on in my spare time," he said, walking around the kitchen while she fixed him a cup of tea. "Maybe you've heard about it. I've been getting people to tape-record lists of words and syllables for me. The men do it up at the house, and the women do it in their homes."

"Oh yes," she said.

"They tell me where they were born," he said, "and every place they've lived and for how long." He walked around, touching cabinet knobs. "I'm going to feed everything into a computer eventually, each tape with its geographical data. With enough samples I'll be able to feed in a tape *without* data"—he ran a fingertip along a counter edge, looking at her with his bright eyes—"maybe even a very *short* tape, a few words or a sentence—and the computer'll be able to give a geographical rundown on the person, where he was born and where he's lived. Sort of an electronic Henry Higgins. Not just a stunt though; I see it as being useful in police work."

She said, "My friend Bobbie Markowe—"

"Dave's wife, sure."

"—got laryngitis from taping for you."

"Because she rushed it," Claude said. "She did the whole thing in two evenings. You don't have to do it that fast. I leave the recorder; you can take as long as you like. Would you? It would be a big help to me."

Walter came in from the patio; he had been burning leaves out in back with Pete and Kim. He and Claude said hello to each other and shook hands. "I'm sorry," he said to Joanna, "I was supposed to tell you Claude was coming to speak to you. Do you think you'll be able to help him?"

She said, "I have so little free time—"

"Do it in odd moments," Claude said. "I don't care if it takes a few *weeks*."

"Well if you don't mind leaving the recorder that long . . ."

"And you get a present in exchange," Claude said, unstrapping his briefcase on the table. "I leave an extra cartridge, you tape any little lullabies or things you like to sing to the kids, and I transcribe them onto a record. If you're out for an evening the sitter can play it."

"Oh, that'd be nice," she said, and Walter said, "You could do 'The Goodnight Song' and 'Good Morning Starshine.' "

"Anything you want," Claude said. "The more the merrier."

"I'd better get back outside," Walter said. "The fire's still burning. See you, Claude."

"Right," Claude said.

Joanna gave Claude his tea, and he showed her how to load and use the tape recorder, a handsome one in a black leather case. He gave her eight yellow-boxed cartridges and a black loose-leaf binder.

"My gosh, there's a lot," she said, leafing through curled and mended pages typed in triple columns.

"It goes quickly," Claude said. "You just say each word clearly in your regular voice and take a little stop before the next one. And see that the needle stays in the red. You want to practice?"

They had Thanksgiving dinner with Walter's brother Dan and his family. It was arranged by Walter and Dan's mother and was meant to be a reconciliation—the brothers had been on the outs for a year because of a dispute about their father's estate—but the dispute flared again, grown in bitterness as the disputed property had grown in value. Walter and Dan shouted, their mother shouted louder, and Joanna made difficult explanations to Pete and Kim in the car going home.

She took pictures of Bobbie's oldest boy Jonathan working with his microscope, and men in a cherry picker trimming trees on Norwood Road. She was trying to get up a portfolio of at least a dozen first-rate photos—to dazzle the agency into a contract.

The first snow fell on a night when Walter was at the Men's Association. She watched it from the den window: a scant powder of glittery white, swirling in the light of the walk lamp-post. Nothing that would amount to anything. But more would come. Fun, good pictures—and the bother of boots and snow-suits.

Across the street, in the Claybrooks' living-room window, Donna Claybrook sat polishing what looked like an athletic trophy, buffing at it with steady mechanical movements. Joanna watched her and shook her head. *They never stop, these Stepford wives*, she thought.

It sounded like the first line of a poem.

They never stop, these Stepford wives. They something something *all their lives.* Work like robots. Yes, that would fit. *They work like robots all their lives.*

She smiled. Try sending *that* to the *Chronicle*.

She went to the desk and sat down and moved the pen she had left as a placemark on the typed page. She listened for a moment—to the silence from upstairs—and switched the recorder on. With a finger to the page, she leaned toward the microphone propped against the framed Ike Mazzard drawing of her. "Taker. Takes. Taking," she said. "Talcum. Talent. Talented. Talk. Talkative. Talked. Talker. Talking. Talks."

2

She would only want to move, she decided, if she found an absolutely perfect house; one that, besides having the right number of right-size rooms, needed practically no redecoration and had an existing dark-room or something darn close to one. And it would have to cost no more than the fifty-two-five they had paid (and could still get, Walter was sure) for the Stepford house.

A tall order, and she wasn't going to waste too much time trying to fill it. But she went out looking with Bobbie one cold bright early-December morning.

Bobbie was looking *every* morning—in Norwood, Eastbridge, and New Sharon. As soon as she found something right—and she was far more flexible in her demands than Joanna—she was going to pressure Dave for an immediate move, despite the boys' having to change schools in the middle of the year. "Better a little disruption in their lives than a zombie-ized mother," she said. She really was drinking bottled water, and wasn't eating any locally grown produce. "You can buy bottled oxygen, you know," Joanna said.

"Screw you. I can see you now, comparing Ajax to your present cleanser."

The looking inclined Joanna to look more; the women they met—Eastbridge homeowners and a real-estate broker named Miss Kirgassa—were alert, lively, and quirky, confirming by contrast the blandness of Stepford women. And Eastbridge offered a wide range of community activities, for women and for men *and* women. There was even a NOW chapter in formation. "Why didn't you look here first?" Miss Kirgassa asked, rocketing her car down a zigzag road at terrifying speed.

"My husband had heard—" Joanna said, clutching the armrest, watching the road, tramping on wished-for brakes.

"It's *dead* there. We're much more with-it."

"We'd like to get back there to pack though," Bobbie said from in back.

Miss Kirgassa brayed a laugh. "I can drive these roads blindfolded," she said. "I want to show you two more places after this one."

On the way back to Stepford, Bobbie said, "That's for me. I'm going to be a broker, I just decided. You get out, you meet people, and you get to look in everyone's closets. And you can set your own hours. I mean it, I'm going to find out what the requirements are."

They got a letter from the Department of Health, two pages long. It assured them that their interest in environmental protection was shared by both their state and county governments. Industrial installations throughout the state were subject to stringent anti-pollutionary regulations such as the following. These were enforced not only by frequent inspection of the installations themselves, but also by regular examination of soil, water, and air samples. There was no indication whatsoever of harmful pollution in the Stepford area, nor of any naturally occurring chemical presence that might produce a tranquilizing or depressant effect. They could rest assured that their concern was groundless, but their letter was appreciated nonetheless.

"Bullshit," Bobbie said, and stayed with the bottled water. She brought a thermos of coffee with her whenever she came to Joanna's.

Walter was lying on his side, facing away from her, when she came out of the bathroom. She sat down on the bed, turned the lamp off, and got in under the blanket. She lay on her back and watched the ceiling take shape over her.

"Walter?" she said.

"Mm?"

"Was that any good?" she asked. "For you?"

"Sure it was," he said. "Wasn't it for you?"

"Yes," she said.

He didn't say anything.

"I've had the feeling that it hasn't been," she said. "Good for you. The last few times."

"No," he said. "It's been fine. Just like always."

She lay seeing the ceiling. She thought of Charmaine, who wouldn't let Ed catch her (or had she changed in *that* too?), and she remembered Bobbie's remark about Dave's odd ideas.

"Good night," Walter said.

"Is there anything," she asked, "that I—don't do that you'd like me to do? Or that I *do* do that you'd like me not to?"

He didn't say anything, and then he said, "Whatever *you* want to do, that's all." He turned over and looked at her, up on his elbow. "Really," he said, and smiled, "it's fine. Maybe I've been a little tired lately because of the commuting." He kissed her cheek. "Go to sleep," he said.

"Are you—having an affair with Esther?"

"Oh for God's sake," he said. "She's going with a *Black Panther*. I'm not having an affair with anybody."

"A Black Panther?"

"That's what Don's secretary told *him*. We don't even *talk* about sex; all I do is correct her spelling. Come on, let's get to sleep." He kissed her cheek and turned away from her.

She turned over onto her stomach and closed her eyes. She shifted and stirred, trying to settle herself comfortably.

.   .   .

They went to a movie in Norwood with Bobbie and Dave, and spent an evening with them in front of the fire, playing Monopoly kiddingly.

A heavy snow fell on a Saturday night, and Walter gave up his Sunday-afternoon football-watching, not very happily, to take Pete and Kim sledding on Winter Hill while she drove to New Sharon and shot a roll and a half of color in a bird sanctuary.

Pete got the lead in his class Christmas play; and Walter, on the way home one night, either lost his wallet or had his pocket picked.

She brought sixteen photos in to the agency. Bob Silverberg, the man she dealt with there, admired them gratifyingly but told her that the agency wasn't signing contracts with *anybody* at that time. He kept the photos, saying he would let her know in a day or two whether he felt any of them were marketable. She had lunch, disappointedly, with an old friend, Doris Lombardo, and did some Christmas shopping for Walter and her parents.

Ten of the pictures came back, including "Off Duty," which she decided at once she would enter in the next *Saturday Review* contest. Among the six the agency had kept and would handle was "Student," the one of Jonny Markowe at his microscope. She called Bobbie and told her. "I'll give him ten per cent of whatever it makes," she said.

"Does that mean we can stop giving him allowance?"

"You'd better not. My best one's made a little over a thousand so far, but the other two have only made about two hundred each."

"Well that's not bad for a kid who looks like Peter Lorre," Bobbie said. "Him I mean, not you. Listen, I was going to call you. Can you take Adam for the weekend? Would you?"

"Sure," she said. "Pete and Kim would love it. Why?"

"Dave's had a brainstorm; we're going to have a weekend alone, just the two of us. Second-honey-moon time."

A sense of beforeness touched her; déjà vu. She brushed it away. "That's great," she said.

"We've got Jonny and Kenny booked in the neighborhood," Bobbie said, "but I thought Adam would have a better time at your place."

"Sure," Joanna said, "it'll make it easier to keep Pete and Kim out of each other's hair. What are you doing, going into the city?"

"No, just staying here. And getting snowed in, we hope. I'll bring him over tomorrow after school, okay? And pick him up late Sunday."

"Fine. How's the house-hunting?"

"Not so good. I saw a beauty in Norwood this morning, but they're not getting out till April first."

"So stick around."

"No, thanks. Want to get together?"

"I can't; I've *got* to do some cleaning. Really."

"You see? You're changing. That Stepford magic is starting to work."

A black woman in an orange scarf and striped fake-fur coat stood waiting at the library desk, her finger-tips resting on a stack of books. She glanced at Joanna and nodded with a near-smile; Joanna nodded and near-smiled back; and the black woman looked away —at the empty chair behind the desk, and the book-shelves behind the chair. She was tall and tan-skinned, with close-cropped black hair and large dark eyes—exotic-looking and attractive. About thirty.

Joanna, going to the desk, took her gloves off and got the postcard out of her pocket. She looked at Miss Austrian's namestand on the desk, and at the books under the long slim fingers of the black woman a few feet away. *A Severed Head* by Iris Murdoch, with *I Know Why the Caged Bird Sings* and *The Magus* under-neath it. Joanna looked at the postcard; Skinner, *Beyond Freedom & Dignity* would be held for her until 12/11. She wanted to say something friendly and wel-coming—the woman was surely the wife or daughter of the black family the Welcome Wagon lady had mentioned—but she didn't want to be white-liberal patronizing. Would she say something if the woman *weren't* black? Yes, in a situation like this she—"We could walk off with the whole place if we wanted to," the black woman said, and Joanna smiled at her and said, "We ought to; teach her to stay on the job." She nodded toward the desk.

The black woman smiled. "Is it always this empty?" she asked.

"I've never seen it *this* way before," Joanna said. "But I've only been here in the afternoon and on Saturdays."

"Are you new in Stepford?"

"Three months."

"Three *days* for me," the black woman said.

"I hope you like it."

"I think I will."

Joanna put her hand out. "I'm Joanna Eberhart," she said, smiling.

"Ruthanne Hendry," the black woman said, smiling and shaking Joanna's hand.

Joanna tipped her head and squinted. "I *know* that name," she said. "I've seen it someplace."

The woman smiled. "Do you have any small children?" she asked.

Joanna nodded, puzzled.

"I've done a children's book, *Penny Has a Plan*," the woman said. "They've got it here; I checked the catalog first thing."

"Of *course*," Joanna said. "Kim had it out about two weeks ago! And loved it! I did too; it's so good to find one where a girl actually *does* something besides make tea for her dolls."

"Subtle propaganda," Ruthanne Hendry said, smiling.

"You did the illustrations too," Joanna said. "They were terrific!"

"Thank you."

"Are you doing another one?"

Ruthanne Hendry nodded. "I've got one laid out," she said. "I'll be starting the real work as soon as we get settled."

"I'm sorry," Miss Austrian said, coming limping from the back of the room. "It's so quiet here in the morning that I"—she stopped and blinked, and came limping on—"work in the office. Have to get one of those bells people can tap on. Hello, Mrs. Eberhart." She smiled at Joanna, and at Ruthanne Hendry.

"Hello," Joanna said. "This is one of your authors. *Penny Has a Plan*. Ruthanne Hendry."

"Oh?" Miss Austrian sat down heavily in the chair and held its arms with plump pink hands. "That's a very popular book," she said. "We have two copies in circulation and they're both replacements."

"I *like* this library," Ruthanne Hendry said. "Can I join?"

"Do you live in Stepford?"

"Yes, I just moved here."

"Then you're welcome to join," Miss Austrian said. She opened a drawer, took out a white card, and put it down beside the stack of books.

At the Center's luncheonette counter, empty except for two telephone repairmen, Ruthanne stirred her

coffee, and looking at Joanna, said, "Tell me something, on the level: was there much reaction to our
buying here?"

"None at all that I heard of," Joanna said. "It's not
a town where reactions can develop—to anything.
There's no place where people really intersect, except
the Men's Association."

"*They're* all right," Ruthanne said. "Royal is joining tomorrow night. But the *women* in the neighborhood—"

"Oh listen," Joanna said, "that doesn't have anything to do with *color*, believe me. They're like that
with everybody. No time for a cup of coffee, right?
Riveted on their housework?"

Ruthanne nodded. "I don't mind for myself," she
said. "I'm very self-sufficient, otherwise I wouldn't
have gone along with the move. But I—"

Joanna told her about the Stepford women, and
how Bobbie was even planning to move away to
avoid becoming like them.

Ruthanne smiled. "There's *nothing* that's going to
make a hausfrau out of *me*," she said. "If *they're* that
way, fine. I was just concerned about it being about
color because of the girls." She had two of them, four
and six; and her husband Royal was chairman of the
sociology department of one of the city universities.
Joanna told her about Walter and Pete and Kim, and
about her photography.

They exchanged phone numbers. "I turned into a
hermit when I was working on *Penny*," Ruthanne
said, "but I'll call you sooner or later."

"I'll call *you*," Joanna said. "If you're busy, just say

so. I want you to meet Bobbie; I'm sure you'll like each other."

On the way to their cars—they had left them in front of the library—Joanna saw Dale Coba looking at her from a distance. He stood with a lamb in his arms, by a group of men setting up a crèche near the Historical Society cottage. She nodded at him, and he, holding the live-looking lamb, nodded and smiled.

She told Ruthanne who he was, and asked her if she knew that Ike Mazzard lived in Stepford.

"Who?"

"Ike Mazzard. The illustrator."

Ruthanne had never heard of him, which made Joanna feel very old. Or very white.

Having Adam for the weekend was a mixed blessing. On Saturday he and Pete and Kim played beautifully together, inside the house and out; but on Sunday, a freezing-cold overcast day when Walter laid claim to the family room for football-watching (fairly enough after last Sunday's sledding), Adam and Pete became, serially, soldiers in a blanket-over-the-dining-table fort, explorers in the cellar ("Stay out of that darkroom!"), and Star Trek people in Pete's room—all of them sharing, strangely enough, a single common enemy called Kim-She's-Dim. They were loudly and scornfully watchful, preparing defenses; and poor Kim *was* dim, wanting only to join them, not to crayon or help file negatives, not even—Joanna was desperate—to bake cookies. Adam and Pete ignored threats, Kim ignored blandishments, Walter ignored everything.

Joanna was glad when Bobbie and Dave came to pick Adam up.

But she was glad she had taken him when she saw how great they looked. Bobbie had had her hair done and was absolutely beautiful—either due to make-up or lovemaking, probably both. And Dave looked jaunty and keyed up and happy. They brought bracing coldness into the entrance hall. "Hi, Joanna, how'd it go?" Dave said, rubbing leather-gloved hands; and Bobbie, wrapped in her raccoon coat, said, "I hope Adam wasn't any trouble."

"Not a speck," Joanna said. "You look marvelous, both of you!"

"We *feel* marvelous," Dave said, and Bobbie smiled and said, "It was a lovely weekend. Thank you for helping us manage it."

"Forget it," Joanna said. "I'm going to plunk Pete with *you* one of these weekends."

"We'll be glad to take him," Bobbie said, and Dave said, "Whenever you want, just say the word. *Adam? Time to go!*"

"He's up in Pete's room."

Dave cupped his gloved hands and shouted, "*Adam! We're here! Get your stuff!*"

"Take your coats off," Joanna said.

"Got to pick up Jon and Kenny," Dave said, and Bobbie said, "I'm sure you'd like some peace and quiet. It must have been hectic."

"Well it hasn't been my most *restful* Sunday," Joanna said. "Yesterday was great though."

"Hi there!" Walter said, coming in from the kitchen with a glass in his hand.

Bobbie said, "Hello, Walter," and Dave said, "Hi, buddy!"

"How was the second honeymoon?" Walter asked.

"Better than the first," Dave said. "Just shorter, that's all." He grinned at Walter.

Joanna looked at Bobbie, expecting her to say something funny. Bobbie smiled at her and looked toward the stairs. "Hello, gumdrop," she said. "Did you have a nice weekend?"

"I don't want to go," Adam said, standing tilted to keep his shopping bag clear of the stair. Pete and Kim stood behind him. Kim said, "Can't he stay another night?"

"No, dear, there's school tomorrow," Bobbie said, and Dave said, "Come on, pal, we've got to collect the rest of the Mafia."

Adam came sulkily down the stairs, and Joanna went to the closet for his coat and boots. "Hey," Dave said, "I've got some information on that stock you asked me about." Walter said, "Oh, good," and he and Dave went into the living room.

Joanna gave Adam's coat to Bobbie, and Bobbie thanked her and held it open for Adam. He put his shopping bag down and winged back his arms to the coat sleeves.

Joanna, holding Adam's boots, said, "Do you want a bag for these?"

"No, don't bother," Bobbie said. She turned Adam around and helped him with his buttons.

"You smell nice," he said.

"Thanks, gumdrop."

He looked at the ceiling and at her. "I don't like you to *call* me that," he said. "I *used* to, but now I don't."

"I'm sorry," she said. "I won't do it again." She smiled at him and kissed him on the forehead.

Walter and Dave came out of the living room, and Adam picked up his shopping bag and said good-by to Pete and Kim. Joanna gave Adam's boots to Bobbie and touched cheeks with her. Bobbie's was still cool from outside, and she *did* smell nice. "Speak to you tomorrow," Joanna said.

"Sure," Bobbie said. They smiled at each other. Bobbie moved to Walter at the door and offered her cheek. He hesitated—Joanna wondered why—and pecked it.

Dave kissed Joanna, clapped Walter on the arm— "So long, buddy"—and steered Adam out after Bobbie.

"Can we go in the family room now?" Pete asked.

"It's all yours," Walter said.

Pete ran away and Kim ran after him.

Joanna and Walter stood at the cold glass of the storm door, looking out at Bobbie and Dave and Adam getting into their car.

"Fantastic," Walter said.

"Don't they look great?" Joanna said. "Bobbie didn't even look that good at the party. Why didn't you want to kiss her?"

Walter didn't say anything, and then he said, "Oh, I don't know, *cheek*-kissing. It's so damn show-business."

"I never noticed you objecting before."

"Then I've changed, I guess," he said.

She watched the car doors close, and its headlights flash on. "How about *us* having a weekend alone?" she said. "They'll take Pete, they said they would, and I'm sure the Van Sants would take Kim."

"That'd be great," he said. "Right after the holidays."

"Or maybe the Hendrys," she said. "*They've* got a six-year-old girl, and I'd like Kim to get to know a black family."

The car pulled away, red taillights shining, and Walter closed the door and locked it and thumbed down the switch of the outside lights. "Want a drink?" he asked.

"And how," Joanna said. "I need one after today."

Ugh, what a Monday: Pete's room to be reassembled and all the others straightened out, the beds to be changed, washing (and she'd let it pile up, of course), tomorrow's shopping list to make up, and three pairs of Pete's pants to be lengthened. That was what she was *doing*; never mind what *else* had to be done—the Christmas shopping, and the Christmas-card addressing, and making Pete's costume for the play (thanks for *that*, Miss Turner). Bobbie didn't call, thank goodness; this wasn't a day for kaffee-klatsching. *Is she right?* Joanna wondered. *Am I changing?* Hell, no; the housework *had* to be caught up with once in a while, otherwise the place would turn into—well, into *Bobbie's* place. Besides, a real Stepford wife would sail through it all very calmly and efficiently, not running the vacuum cleaner over its cord and then mashing her fingers getting the cord out from around the damn roller thing.

She gave Pete hell about not putting toys away when he was done playing with them, and he sulked for an hour and wouldn't talk to her. And Kim was coughing.

And Walter begged off his turn at K.P. and ran out to get into Herb Sundersen's full car. Busy time at the Men's Association; the Christmas-Toys project. (Who for? Were there needy children in Stepford? She'd seen no sign of any.)

She cut a sheet to start Pete's costume, a snowman, and played a game of Concentration with him and Kim (who only coughed once but keep the fingers crossed); and then she addressed Christmas cards down through the L's and went to bed at ten. She fell asleep with the Skinner book.

Tuesday was better. When she had cleaned up the breakfast mess and made the beds, she called Bobbie —no answer; she was house-hunting—and drove to the Center and did the week's main marketing. She went to the Center again after lunch, took pictures of the crèche, and got home just ahead of the school bus.

Walter did the dishes and *then* went to the Men's Association. The toys were for kids in the city, ghetto kids and kids in hospitals. Complain about *that*, Ms. Eberhart. Or would she still be Ms. Ingalls? Ms. Ingalls-Eberhart?

After she got Pete and Kim bathed and into bed she called Bobbie. It was odd that Bobbie hadn't called *her* in two full days. "Hello?" Bobbie said.

"Long time no speak."

"Who's this?"

"Joanna."

"Oh, hello," Bobbie said. "How are you?"

"Fine. Are you? You sound sort of blah."

"No, I'm fine," Bobbie said.

"Any luck this morning?"

"What do you mean?"

"House-hunting."

"I went shopping this morning," Bobbie said.

"Why didn't you call me?"

"I went very early."

"I went around ten; we must have just missed each other."

Bobbie didn't say anything.

"Bobbie?"

"Yes?"

"Are you *sure* you're okay?"

"Positive. I'm in the middle of some ironing."

"At this hour?"

"Dave needs a shirt for tomorrow."

"Oh. Call me in the morning then; maybe we can have lunch. Unless you're going house-hunting."

"I'm not," Bobbie said.

"Call me then, okay?"

"Okay," Bobbie said. " 'By, Joanna."

"Good-by."

She hung up and sat looking at the phone and her hand on it. The thought struck her—ridiculously—that Bobbie had changed the way Charmaine had. No, not Bobbie; impossible. She must have had a fight with Dave, a major one that she wasn't ready to talk about yet. Or could she herself have offended Bobbie in some way without being aware of it? Had she said something Sunday about Adam's stay-over that Bobbie might have misinterpreted? But no, they'd parted as friendly as ever, touching cheeks and saying they'd speak to each other. (Yet even then, now that she thought about it, Bobbie had seemed different; she—hadn't said the sort of things she usually did, and she'd moved more slowly too.) Maybe she and Dave had been smoking pot over the weekend. They'd tried it a couple of times without much effect, Bobbie had said. Maybe this time . . .

She addressed a few Christmas cards.

She called Ruthanne Hendry, who was friendly and glad to hear from her. They talked about *The Magus*, which Ruthanne was enjoying as much as Joanna had, and Ruthanne told her about her new book, another Penny story. They agreed to have lunch together the following week. Joanna would speak to Bobbie, and the three of them would go to the French place in Eastbridge. Ruthanne would call her Monday morning.

She addressed Christmas cards, and read the Skinner book in bed until Walter came home. "I spoke to Bobbie tonight," she said. "She sounded—different, washed out."

"She's probably tired from all that running around she's been doing," Walter said, emptying his jacket pockets onto the bureau.

"She seemed different Sunday too," Joanna said. "She didn't say—"

"She had some make-up on, that's all," Walter said. "You're not going to start in with that chemical business, are you?"

She frowned, pressing the closed book to her blanketed knees. "Did Dave say anything about their trying pot again?" she asked.

"No," Walter said, "but maybe that's the answer."

They made love, but she was tense and couldn't really give herself, and it wasn't very good.

Bobbie didn't call. Around one o'clock Joanna drove over. The dogs barked at her as she got out of the station wagon. They were chained to an overhead line behind the house, the corgi up on his hind legs, pawing air and yipping, the sheepdog standing shaggy and stock-still, barking "Ruff, ruff, ruff, ruff, ruff." Bobbie's blue Chevy stood in the driveway.

Bobbie, in her immaculate living room—cushions all fluffed, woodwork gleaming, magazines fanned on the polished table behind the sofa—smiled at Joanna and said, "I'm sorry, I was so busy it slipped my mind. Have you had lunch? Come on into the kitchen. I'll fix you a sandwich. What would you like?"

She looked the way she had on Sunday—beautiful, her hair done, her face made-up. And she was wearing some kind of padded high-uplift bra under her green sweater, and a hip-whittling girdle under the brown pleated skirt.

In her immaculate kitchen she said, "Yes, I've changed. I realized I was being awfully sloppy and self-indulgent. It's no disgrace to be a good home-maker. I've decided to do my job conscientiously, the way Dave does his, and to be more careful about my appearance. Are you sure you don't want a sandwich?"

Joanna shook her head. *"Bobbie,"* she said, *"I— Don't you see what's happened? Whatever's around here—it's got you, the way it got Charmaine!"*

Bobbie smiled at her. "Nothing's got me," she said. "There's nothing around. That was a lot of nonsense. Stepford's a fine healthful place to live."

"You—don't want to move any more?"

"Oh no," Bobbie said. "That was nonsense too. I'm perfectly happy here. Can't I at least make you a cup of coffee?"

She called Walter at his office. "Oh good ahfter*noon!*" Esther said. "*So* nice to speak to you! It must be a *super* day up there, or are you *hyar* in town?"

"No, I'm at home," she said. "May I speak to Walter, please?"

"I'm afraid he's in conference at the moment."

"It's important. Please tell him."

"Hold on a sec then."

She held on, sitting at the den desk, looking at the papers and envelopes she had taken from the center drawer, and at the calendar—*Tue. Dec. 14,* yesterday— and the Ike Mazzard drawing.

"He'll be right with you, Mrs. Eberhart," Esther said. "Nothing wrong with Peter or Kim, I hope."

"No, they're fine."

"Good. They must be having a—"

"Hello?" Walter said.

"Walter?"

"Hello. What is it?"

"Walter, I want you to listen to me and don't argue," she said. "Bobbie *has* changed. I was over there. The house looks like— It's *spotless,* Walter; it's *immaculate*! And she's got herself all— Listen, do you have the bankbooks? I've been looking for them and I can't find them. Walter?"

"Yes, I've got them," he said. "I've been buying some stock, on Dave's recommendations. What do you want them for?"

"To see what we've got," she said. "There was a house I saw in Eastbridge that—"

"Joanna."

"—was a little more than this one but—"

"Joanna, listen to me."

"I'm not going to stay here another—"

"Listen to me, damn it!"

She gripped the handset. "Go ahead," she said.

"I'll try to get home early," he said. "Don't do anything till I get there. You hear me? Don't make any commitments or anything. I think I can get away in about half an hour."

"I'm not going to stay here another day," she said.

"Just wait till I get there, will you?" he said. "We can't talk about this on the phone."

"Bring the bankbooks," she said.

"Don't do anything till I get there." The phone clicked dead.

She hung up.

She put the papers and envelopes back into the center drawer and closed it. Then she got the phone book from the shelf and looked up Miss Kirgassa's number in Eastbridge.

The house she was thinking of, the St. Martin house, was still on the market. "In fact I think they've come down a bit since you saw it."

"Would you do me a favor?" she said. "We may be interested; I'll know definitely tomorrow. Would you find out the rock-bottom price they'll take for an immediate sale, and let me know as soon as you can?"

"I'll get right back to you," Miss Kirgassa said. "Do you know if Mrs. Markowe has found something? We had an appointment this morning but she didn't show up."

"She changed her mind, she's not moving," she said. "But I am."

She called Buck Raymond, the broker they'd used in Stepford. "Just hypothetically," she said, "if we were to put the house on the market tomorrow, do you think we could sell it quickly?"

"No doubt about it," Buck said. "There's a steady

demand here. I'm sure you could get what you paid, maybe even a little more. Aren't you happy in it?"

"No," she said.

"I'm sorry to hear that. Shall I start showing it? There's a couple here right now who are—"

"No, no, not yet," she said. "I'll let you know tomorrow."

"Now just hold on a minute," Walter said, making spread-handed calming gestures.

"No," she said, shaking her head. "No. Whatever it is takes four months to work, which means I've got one more month to go. Maybe less; we moved here September fourth."

"For God's sake, Joanna—"

"Charmaine moved here in July," she said. "She changed in November. Bobbie moved here in August and now it's December." She turned and walked away from him. The sink's faucet was leaking; she hit the handle back hard and the leaking stopped.

"You *had* the letter from the Department of Health," Walter said.

"Bullshit, to quote Bobbie." She turned and faced him. "There's *something*, there's *got* to be," she said. "Go take a look. Would you do that, please? She's got her bust shoved out to here, and her behind girdled down to practically nothing! The house is like a commercial. Like Carol's, and Donna's, and Kit Sundersen's!"

"She had to clean it sooner or later; it was a pig-sty."

"She's *changed*, Walter! She doesn't *talk* the same, she doesn't *think* the same—and I'm not going to wait around for it to happen to me!"

"We're not going to—"

Kim came in from the patio, her face red in its fur-edged hood.

"Stay out, Kim," Walter said.

"We want some supplies," Kim said. "We're going on a hike."

Joanna went to the cookie jar and opened it and got out cookies. "Here," she said, putting them into Kim's mittened hands. "Stay near the house, it's getting dark."

"Can we have Oreos?"

"We don't *have* Oreos. Go on."

Kim went out. Walter closed the door.

Joanna brushed crumbs from her hand. "It's a nicer house than this one," she said, "and we can have it for fifty-three-five. And we can get that for this one; Buck Raymond said so."

"We're not moving," Walter said.

"You *said* we would!"

"Next summer, not—"

"I won't be *me* next summer!"

"Joanna—"

"Don't you understand? It's going to happen to *me*, in *January*!"

"*Nothing's* going to happen to you!"

"That's what I told Bobbie! I kidded her about the bottled water!"

He came close to her. "There's nothing in the water, there's nothing in the air," he said. "They changed for exactly the reasons they told you: because they realized they'd been lazy and negligent. If Bobbie's taking an interest in her appearance, it's about time. It wouldn't hurt *you* to look in a mirror once in a while."

She looked at him, and he looked away, flushing, and looked back at her. "I mean it," he said. "You're a very pretty woman and you don't do a damn thing with yourself any more unless there's a party or something."

He turned away from her and went and stood at the stove. He twisted a knob one way and the other.

She looked at him.

He said, "I'll tell you what we'll do—"

"Do you *want* me to change?" she asked.

"Of course not, don't be silly." He turned around.

"Is *that* what you want?" she asked. "A cute little gussied-up hausfrau?"

"All I said was—"

"Is *that* why Stepford was the only place to move? Did somebody pass the message to you? 'Take her to Stepford, Wally old pal; there's something in the air there; she'll change in four months.'"

"There's nothing in the air," Walter said. "The message I got was good schools and low taxes. Now look, I'm trying to see this from your viewpoint and make some kind of fair judgment. You want to move because you're afraid you're going to 'change'; and I think you're being irrational and—a little hysterical, and that moving at this point would impose an undue

hardship on all of us, especially Pete and Kim." He
stopped and drew a breath. "All right, let's do this,"
he said. "You have a talk with Alan Hollingsworth,
and if he says you're—"

"With who?"

"Alan Hollingsworth," he said. His eyes went
from hers. "The psychiatrist. You know." His eyes
came back. "If he says you're not going through
some—"

"I don't need a psychiatrist," she said. "And if I
did, I wouldn't want Alan Hollingsworth. I saw his
wife at the P.T.A.; she's one of *them*. You *bet* he'd
think I'm irrational."

"Then pick someone else," he said. "Anyone you
want. If you're not going through some kind of—
delusion or something, then we'll move, as soon as we
possibly can. I'll look at that house tomorrow morning, and even put a deposit on it."

"I don't need a psychiatrist," she said. "I need to
get out of Stepford."

"Now come on, Joanna," he said. "I think I'm being damn fair. You're asking us to undergo a major
upheaval, and I think you owe it to all of us, including yourself—*especially* yourself—to make sure you're
seeing things as clearly as you think you are."

She looked at him.

"Well?" he said.

She didn't say anything. She looked at him.

"Well?" he said. "Doesn't that sound reasonable?"

She said, "Bobbie changed when she was alone
with Dave, and Charmaine changed when she was
alone with Ed."

He looked away, shaking his head.

"Is that when it's going to happen to *me*?" she asked. "On *our* weekend alone?"

"It was *your idea*," he said.

"Would *you* have suggested it if *I* hadn't?"

"Now you *see*?" he said. "Do you hear how you're talking? I want you to think about what I said. You can't disrupt all our lives on the spur of the moment this way. It's unreasonable to expect to." He turned around and went out of the kitchen.

She stood there, and put her hand to her forehead and closed her eyes. She stayed that way, and then lowered her hand, opened her eyes, and shook her head. She went to the refrigerator and opened it, and took out a covered bowl and a market-pack of meat.

He sat at the desk, writing on a yellow pad. A cigarette in the ashtray ribboned smoke up into the lamplight. He looked at her and took his glasses off.

"All right," she said. "I'll—speak to someone. But a woman."

"Good," he said. "That's a good idea."

"And you'll put a deposit on the house tomorrow?"

"Yes," he said. "Unless there's something radically wrong with it."

"There isn't," she said. "It's a good house and it's only six years old. With a good mortgage."

"Fine," he said.

She stood looking at him. "*Do* you want me to change?" she asked him.

"No," he said. "I'd just like you to put on a little lipstick once in a while. That's no big change. I'd like *me* to change a little too, like lose a few pounds for instance."

She pushed her hair back straight. "I'm going to work down in the darkroom for a while," she said. "Pete's still awake. Will you keep an ear open?"

"Sure," he said, and smiled at her.

She looked at him, and turned and went away.

She called the good old Department of Health, and they referred her to the county medical society, and *they* gave her the names and phone numbers of five women psychiatrists. The two nearest ones, in East-bridge, were booked solid through mid-January; but the third, in Sheffield, north of Norwood, could see her on Saturday afternoon at two. Dr. Margaret Fancher; she sounded nice over the phone.

She finished the Christmas cards, and Pete's costume; bought toys and books for Pete and Kim, and a bottle of champagne for Bobbie and Dave. She had gotten a gold belt buckle for Walter in the city, and had planned to canvass the Route Nine antique stores for legal documents; instead she bought him a tan cardigan.

The first Christmas cards came in—from her parents and Walter's junior partners, from the Mc-

Cormicks, the Chamalians, and the Van Sants. She lined them up on a living-room bookshelf.

A check came from the agency: a hundred and twenty-five dollars.

On Friday afternoon, despite two inches of snow and more falling, she put Pete and Kim into the station wagon and drove over to Bobbie's.

Bobbie welcomed them pleasantly; Adam and Kenny and the dogs welcomed them noisily. Bobbie made hot chocolate, and Joanna carried the tray into the family room. "Watch your step," Bobbie said, "I waxed the floor this morning."

"I noticed," Joanna said.

She sat in the kitchen watching Bobbie—beautiful, shapely Bobbie—cleaning the oven with paper towels and a spray can of cleaner. "What have you *done* to yourself, for God's sake?" she asked.

"I'm not eating the way I used to," Bobbie said. "And I'm getting more exercise."

"You must have lost ten pounds!"

"No, just two or three. I'm wearing a girdle."

"Bobbie, will you *please* tell me what *happened* last weekend?"

"Nothing happened. We stayed in."

"Did you smoke anything, take anything? Drugs, I mean."

"No. Don't be silly."

"Bobbie, you're not *you* any more! Can't you see that? You've become like the others!"

"Honestly, Joanna, that's nonsense," Bobbie said. "Of course I'm me. I simply realized that I was awfully sloppy and self-indulgent, and now I'm doing my job conscientiously, the way Dave does his."

"I know, I know," she said. "How does *he* feel about it?"

"He's very happy."

"I'll bet he is."

"This stuff really works. Do you use it?"

I'm not crazy, she thought. *I'm not crazy.*

Jonny and two other boys were making a snow-man in front of the house next door. She left Pete and Kim in the station wagon and went over and said hello to him. "Oh, hi!" he said. "Do you have any money for me?"

"Not yet," she said, shielding her face against the downfall of thick flakes. "Jonny, I—I can't get over the way your mother's changed."

"Hasn't she?" he said, nodding, panting.

"I can't understand it," she said.

"Neither can I," he said. "She doesn't shout any-more, she makes hot breakfasts . . ." He looked over at the house and frowned. Snowflakes clung to his face. "I hope it lasts," he said, "but I bet it doesn't."

Dr. Fancher was a small elfin-faced woman in her early fifties, with short swirls of graying brown hair, a sharp marionette nose, and smiling blue-gray eyes. She wore a dark blue dress, a gold pin engraved with the Chinese Yang-and-Yin symbol, and a wedding ring. Her office was cheerful, with Chippendale furniture and Paul Klee prints, and striped curtains translucent against the brightness of sun and snow outside. There was a brown leather couch with a paper-covered headrest, but Joanna sat in the chair facing the mahogany desk, on which dozens of small white papers flag-edged the sides of a green blotter.

She said, "I'm here at my husband's suggestion. We moved to Stepford early in September, and I want to move away as soon as possible. We've put a deposit on a house in Eastbridge, but only because I insisted on it. He feels I'm—being irrational."

She told Dr. Fancher why she wanted to move: about Stepford women, and how Charmaine and then Bobbie had changed and become like them. "Have you been to Stepford?" she asked.

"Only once," Dr. Fancher said. "I heard that it was worth looking at, which it is. I've also heard that it's an insular, unsocial community."

"Which it is, believe me."

Dr. Fancher knew of the city in Texas with the low crime rate. "Lithium is what's doing it, apparently," she said. "There was a paper about it in one of the journals."

"Bobbie and I wrote to the Department of Health," Joanna said. "They said there was nothing in Stepford that could be affecting anyone. I suppose they thought we were crackpots. At the time, actually, I thought *Bobbie*—was being a little overanxious. I only helped with the letter because she asked me to . . ." She looked at her clasped hands and worked them against each other.

Dr. Fancher stayed silent.

"I've begun to suspect—" Joanna said. "Oh Jesus, 'suspect'; that sounds so—" She worked her hands together, looking at them.

Dr. Fancher said, "Begun to suspect what?"

She drew her hands apart and wiped them on her skirt. "I've begun to suspect that the men are behind it," she said. She looked at Dr. Fancher.

Dr. Fancher didn't smile or seem surprised. "Which men?" she asked.

Joanna looked at her hands. "My husband," she said. "Bobbie's husband, Charmaine's." She looked at Dr. Fancher. "All of them," she said.

She told her about the Men's Association.

"I was taking pictures in the Center one night a couple of months ago," she said. "That's where those Colonial shops are; the house overlooks them. The windows were open and there was—a smell in the air. Of medicine, or chemicals. And then the shades were pulled down, maybe because they knew I was out there; this policeman had seen me, he stopped and talked to me." She leaned forward. "There are a lot of sophisticated industrial plants on Route Nine," she said, "and a lot of the men who have high-level jobs in them live in Stepford and belong to the Men's Association. *Something* goes on there every night, and I don't think it's just fixing toys for needy children, and pool and poker. There's AmeriChem-Willis, and Stevenson Biochemical. They could be—concocting something that the Department of Health wouldn't know about, up there at the Men's Association . . ." She sat back in the chair, wiping her hands against her skirted thighs, not looking at Dr. Fancher.

Dr. Fancher asked her questions about her family background and her interest in photography; about the jobs she had held, and about Walter and Pete and Kim.

"Any move is traumatic to a degree," Dr. Fancher said, "and particularly the city-to-the-suburbs move for a woman who doesn't find her housewife's role totally fulfilling. It can feel pretty much like being sent to Siberia." She smiled at Joanna. "And the holiday season doesn't help matters any," she said. "It tends to magnify anxieties, for everyone. I've often thought that one year we should have a *real* holiday and skip the whole business."

Joanna made a smile.

Dr. Fancher leaned forward, and joining her hands, rested her elbows on the desk. "I can understand your not being happy in a town of highly home-oriented women," she said to Joanna. "*I* wouldn't be either; no woman with outside interests would. But I do wonder—and I imagine your husband does too—whether you would be happy in Eastbridge, or anywhere else at this particular time."

"I think I would be," Joanna said.

Dr. Fancher looked at her hands, pressing and flexing the wedding-ringed one with the other. She looked at Joanna. "Towns develop their character gradually," she said, "as people pick and choose among them. A few artists and writers came here to Sheffield a long time ago; others followed, and people who found them too Bohemian moved away. Now we're an artists-and-writers town; not exclusively, of course, but enough to make us different from Norwood and Kimball. I'm sure Stepford developed its character in the same way. That seems to me far more likely than the idea that the men there have banded together to chemically brainwash the women. And could they really do it? They could tranquilize them, yes; but these women don't sound tranquilized to me; they're hard-working and industrious within their own small range of interests. That would be quite a job for even the most advanced chemists."

Joanna said, "I know it sounds—" She rubbed her temple.

"It sounds," Dr. Fancher said, "like the idea of a woman who, like many women today, and with good reason, feels a deep resentment and suspicion of men. One who's pulled two ways by conflicting demands, perhaps more strongly than she's aware; the old conventions on the one hand, and the *new* conventions of the liberated woman on the other."

Joanna, shaking her head, said, "If only you could see what Stepford women are *like*. They're actresses in TV commercials, all of them. No, not even *that*. They're—they're like—" She sat forward. "There was a program four or five weeks ago," she said. "My children were watching it. These figures of all the Presidents, moving around, making different facial expressions. Abraham Lincoln stood up and delivered the Gettysburg Address; he was so lifelike you'd have—" She sat still.

Dr. Fancher waited, and nodded. "Rather than force an immediate move on your family," she said, "I think you should con—"

"Disneyland," Joanna said. "The program was from *Disneyland* . . ."

Dr. Fancher smiled. "I know," she said. "My grandchildren were there last summer. They told me they 'met' Lincoln."

Joanna turned from her, staring.

"I think you should consider trying therapy," Dr. Fancher said. "To identify and clarify your feelings. Then you can make the *right* move—maybe to Eastbridge, maybe back to the city; maybe you'll even find Stepford less oppressive."

Joanna turned to her.

"Will you think about it for a day or two and call me?" Dr. Fancher said. "I'm sure I can help you. It's certainly worth a few hours' exploration, isn't it?"

Joanna sat still, and nodded.

Dr. Fancher took a pen from its holder and wrote on a prescription pad.

Joanna looked at her. She stood up and took her handbag from the desk.

"These will help you in the meantime," Dr. Fancher said, writing. "They're a mild tranquilizer. You can take three a day." She tore off a slip and offered it to Joanna, smiling. "They *won't* make you fascinated with housework," she said.

Joanna took the slip.

Dr. Fancher stood up. "I'll be away Christmas week," she said, "but we could start the week of the third. Will you call me Monday or Tuesday and let me know what you've decided?"

Joanna nodded.

Dr. Fancher smiled. "It's *not* catastrophic," she

said. "Really, I'm sure I can help you." She held out her hand.

Joanna shook it and went out.

The library was busy. Miss Austrian said they were down in the cellar. The door on the left, the bottom shelf. Put them back in their proper order. No smoking. Put out the lights.

She went down the steep narrow stairs, touching the wall with one hand. There was no banister.

The door on the left. She found the light switch inside. An eye-sting of fluorescence; the smell of old paper; the whine of a motor, climbing in pitch.

The room was small and low-ceilinged. Walls of shelved magazines surrounded a library table and four kitchen chairs, chrome and red plastic.

Big brown-bound volumes jutted from the bottom shelf all around the room, lying flat, piled six high.

She put her handbag on the table, and took her coat off and laid it over one of the chairs.

She started five years back, leafing backward through the half-a-year volume.

CIVIC AND MEN'S ASSOCIATIONS TO MERGE. The proposed union of the Stepford Civic Association and the Stepford Men's Association has been endorsed by the members of both organizations and will take place within weeks. Thomas C. Miller III and Dale Coba, the respective presidents . . .

She leafed back, through Little League ball games

and heavy snowfalls, through thefts, collisions, school-bond disputes.

WOMEN'S CLUB SUSPENDS MEETINGS. The Stepford Women's Club is suspending its bi-weekly meetings because of declining membership, according to Mrs. Richard Ockrey, who assumed the club's presidency only two months ago on the resignation of former president Mrs. Alan Hollingsworth. "It's only a temporary suspension," Mrs. Ockrey said in her home on Fox Hollow Lane. "We're planning a full-scale membership drive and a resumption of meetings in the early spring . . ."

Do tell, Mrs. Ockrey.

She leafed back through ads for old movies and low-priced food, through a fire at the Methodist Church and the opening of the incinerator plant.

MEN'S ASSOCIATION BUYS TERHUNE HOUSE. Dale Coba, president of the Stepford . . .

A zoning-law change, a burglary at CompuTech.

She dropped the next-earlier volume down onto the other one. Sitting, she opened the volume at its back.

LEAGUE OF WOMEN VOTERS MAY CLOSE.

So what's so surprising about that?

Unless the recent fall-off in membership is reversed, the Stepford League of Women Voters may be forced to close its doors. So warns the league's new president, Mrs. Theodore Van Sant of Fairview Lane . . .

Carol?

Back, back.

A drought was relieved, a drought grew worse.

MEN'S ASSOCIATION RE-ELECTS COBA. Dale

Coba of Anvil Road was elected by acclamation to a second two-year term as president of the steadily expanding . . .

Back two years then.

She jumped three volumes.

A theft, a fire, a bazaar, a snowfall.

She flipped up the pages with one hand, turned them with the other; quickly, quickly.

MEN'S ASSOCIATION FORMED. A dozen Stepford men who repaired the disused barn on Switzer Lane and have been meeting in it for over a year, have formed the Stepford Men's Association and will welcome new members. Dale Coba of Anvil Road has been elected president of the association, Duane T. Anderson of Switzer Lane is vice-president, and Robert Sumner Jr. of Gwendolyn Lane is secretary-treasurer. The purpose of the association, Mr. Coba says, is "strictly social—poker, man-talk, and the pooling of information on crafts and hobbies." The Coba family seems especially apt at getting things started; Mrs. Coba was among the founders of the Stepford Women's Club, although she recently withdrew from it, as did Mrs. Anderson and Mrs. Sumner. Other men in the Stepford Men's Association are Claude Axhelm, Peter J. Duwicki, Frank Ferretti, Steven Margolies, Ike Mazzard, Frank Roddenberry, James J. Scofield, Herbert Sundersen, and Martin I. Weiner. Men interested in further information should . . .

She jumped two more volumes, and now she turned pages in whole-issue clusters, finding each "Notes on Newcomers" in its page-two box.

. . . Mr. Ferretti is an engineer in the systems development laboratory of the CompuTech Corporation.

. . . Mr. Sumner, who holds many patents in dyes and

plastics, recently joined the AmeriChem-Willis Corporation, where he is doing research in vinyl polymers.

"Notes on Newcomers," "Notes on Newcomers"; stopping only when she saw one of the names, skipping to the end of the article, telling herself she was right, she was right.

. . . Mr. Duwicki, known to his friends as Wick, is in the Instatron Corporation's microcircuitry department.

. . . Mr. Weiner is with the Sono-Trak division of the Instatron Corporation.

. . . Mr. Margolies is with Reed & Saunders, the makers of stabilizing devices whose new plant on Route Nine begins operation next week.

She put volumes back, took other volumes out, dropping them heavily on the table.

. . . Mr. Roddenberry is associate chief of the CompuTech Corporation's systems development laboratory.

. . . Mr. Sundersen designs optical sensors for Ulitz Optics, Inc.

And finally she found it.

She read the whole article.

New neighbors on Anvil Road are Mr. and Mrs. Dale Coba and their sons Dale Jr., four, and Darren, two. The Cobas have come here from Anaheim, California, where they lived for six years. "So far we like this part of the country," Mrs. Coba says. "I don't know how we'll feel when winter comes. We're not used to cold weather."

Mr. and Mrs. Coba attended U.C.L.A., and Mr. Coba did postgraduate work at the California Institute of Technology. For the past six years he worked in "audioanimatronics" at Disneyland, helping to create the moving and talking presidential figures featured in the August number of National Geographic. *His hobbies are hunting and piano-playing. Mrs. Coba, who majored in languages, is using her spare time to write a translation of the classic Norwegian novel* The Commander's Daughters.

Mr. Coba's work here will probably be less attention-getting than his work at Disneyland; he has joined the research and development department of Burnham-Massey-Microtech.

She giggled.

Research and development! And *probably less attention-getting*!

She giggled and giggled.

Couldn't stop.

Didn't *want* to!

She laughed, standing up and looking at that "Notes on Newcomers" in its neat box of lines. *PROBABLY be less attention-getting!* Dear God in heaven!

She closed the big brown volume, laughing, and picked it up with a volume beneath it and swung them down to their place on the shelf.

"Mrs. Eberhart?" Miss Austrian upstairs. "It's five of six; we're closing."

Stop laughing, for God's sake. "I'm done!" she called. "I'm just putting them away!"

"Be sure you put them back in the right order."

"I will!" she called.

"And put the lights out."

"Jawohl!"

She put all the volumes away, in their right order more or less. "Oh God in heaven!" she said, giggling. *"Probably!"*

She took her coat and handbag, and switched the lights off, and went giggling up the stairs toward Miss Austrian peering at her. No wonder!

"Did you find what you were looking for?" Miss Austrian asked.

"Oh yes," she said, swallowing the giggles. "Thank you very much. You're a fount of knowledge, you and your library. Thank you. Good night."

"Good night," Miss Austrian said.

She went across to the pharmacy, because God knows she *needed* a tranquilizer. The pharmacy was closing too; half dark, and nobody there but the Cornells. She gave the prescription to Mr. Cornell, and he read it and said, "Yes, you can have this now." He went into the back.

She looked at combs on a rack, smiling. Glass clinked behind her and she turned around.

Mrs. Cornell stood at the wall behind the side counter, outside the lighted part of the pharmacy. She wiped something with a cloth, wiped at the wall shelf, and put the something on it, clinking glass. She was tall and blond, long-legged, full-bosomed; as pretty as—oh, say an Ike Mazzard girl. She took something from the shelf and wiped it, and wiped at the shelf, and put the something on it, clinking glass; and took something from the shelf and—

"Hi there," Joanna said.

Mrs. Cornell turned her head. "Mrs. Eberhart," she said, and smiled. "Hello. How are you?"

"Just fine," Joanna said. "Jim-dandy. How are *you*?"

"Very well, thank you," Mrs. Cornell said. She wiped what she was holding, and wiped at the shelf, and put the something on it, clinking glass; and took something from the shelf and wiped it—

"You do that well," Joanna said.

"It's just dusting," Mrs. Cornell said, wiping at the shelf.

A typewriter peck-peck-pecked from in back. Joanna said, "Do you know the Gettysburg Address?"

"I'm afraid not," Mrs. Cornell said, wiping something.

"Oh come on," Joanna said. "Everybody does. 'Four-score and seven years ago—' "

"I know that but I don't know the rest of it," Mrs. Cornell said. She put the something on the shelf, clinking glass, and took something from the shelf and wiped it.

"Oh, I see, not necessary," Joanna said. "Do you know 'This Little Piggy Went to Market'?"

"Of course," Mrs. Cornell said, wiping at the shelf.

"Charge?" Mr. Cornell asked. Joanna turned. He held out a small white-capped bottle.

"Yes," she said, taking it. "Do you have some water? I'd like to take one now."

He nodded and went in back.

Standing there with the bottle in her hand, she began to tremble. Glass clinked behind her. She pulled the cap from the bottle and pinched out the fluff of cotton. White tablets were inside; she tipped one into her palm, trembling, and pushed the cotton into the bottle and pressed the cap on. Glass clinked behind her.

Mr. Cornell came with a paper cup of water.

"Thank you," she said, taking it. She put the tablet on her tongue and drank and swallowed.

Mr. Cornell was writing on a pad. The top of his head was white scalp, like an under-a-rock *thing*, a slug, with a few strands of brown hair pasted across it. She drank the rest of the water, put the cup down, and put the bottle into her handbag. Glass clinked behind her.

Mr. Cornell turned the pad toward her and offered his pen, smiling. He was ugly; small-eyed, chinless.

She took the pen. "You have a lovely wife," she said, signing the pad. "Pretty, helpful, submissive to her lord and master; you're a lucky man." She held the pen out to him.

He took it, pink-faced. "I know," he said, looking downward.

"This town is full of lucky men," she said. "Good night."

"Good night," he said.

"Good night," Mrs. Cornell said. "Come again."

She went out into the Christmas-lighted street. A few cars passed by, their tires squishing.

The Men's Association windows were alight; and windows of houses farther up the hill. Red, green, and orange twinkled in some of them.

She breathed the night air deeply, and stomped

boot-footed through a snowbank and crossed the street.

She walked down to the floodlit crèche and stood looking at it; at Mary and Joseph and the Infant, and the lambs and calves around them. Very lifelike it all was, though a mite Disneyish.

"Do *you* talk too?" she asked Mary and Joseph.

No answer; they just kept smiling.

She stood there—she wasn't trembling any more—and then she walked back toward the library.

She got into the car, started it, and turned on the lights; and cut across the street, backed, and drove past the crèche and up the hill.

The door opened as she came up the walk, and Walter said, "Where have you been?"

She kicked her boots against the doorstep. "The library," she said.

"Why didn't you *call*? I thought you had an accident, with the snow . . ."

"The roads are clear," she said, scuffing her boots on the mat.

"You should have called, for God's sake. It's after six."

She went in. He closed the door.

She put her handbag on the chair and began taking her gloves off.

"What's she like?" he asked.

"She's very nice," she said. "Sympathetic."

"What did she say?"

She put the gloves into her pockets and began unbuttoning her coat. "She thinks I need a little therapy," she said. "To sort out my feelings before we move. I'm 'pulled two ways by conflicting demands.'" She took the coat off.

"Well that sounds like sensible advice," he said. "To me, anyway. How does it sound to you?"

She looked at the coat, holding it by the lining at its collar, and let it drop over the handbag and the chair. Her hands were cold; she rubbed them palm against palm, looking at them.

She looked at Walter. He was watching her attentively, his head cocked. Stubble sanded his cheeks and darkened his chin-cleft. His face was fuller than she had thought—he was gaining weight—and below his wonderfully blue eyes pouches of flesh had begun to form. How old was he now? Forty on his next birthday, March third.

"To me," she said, "it sounds like a mistake, a very big mistake." She lowered her hands and palmed her skirted sides. "I'm taking Pete and Kim into the city," she said. "To Shep and—"

"What for?"

"—Sylvia's or to a hotel. I'll call you in a day or two. Or have someone call you. Another lawyer."

He stared at her, and said, "What are you *talking* about?"

"I *know*," she said. "I've been reading old *Chronicles*. I know what Dale Coba *used* to do, and I know what he's doing *now*, he and those other—CompuTech Instatron geniuses."

He stared at her, and blinked. "I don't know what you're talking about," he said.

"Oh cut it out." She turned away and went down the hallway and into the kitchen, switching on the lights. The port to the family room showed darkness. She turned; Walter stood in the doorway. "I haven't the foggiest idea what you're talking about," he said.

She strode past him. "Stop lying," she said. "You've been lying to me ever since I took my first picture." She swung around and started up the stairs. "Pete!" she called. "Kim!"

"They're not here."

She looked at him over the banister as he came from the hallway. "When you didn't show up," he said, "I thought it would be a good idea to get them out for the night. In case anything was wrong."

She turned, looking down at him. "Where are they?" she asked.

"With friends," he said. "They're fine."

"*Which* friends?"

He came around to the foot of the stairs. "They're fine," he said.

She turned to face him, found the banister, held it. "Our weekend alone?" she said.

"I think you ought to lie down awhile," he said. He put a hand to the wall, his other hand to the banister. "You're not making sense, Joanna," he said. "Diz, of all people; where does *he* come into things? And what you just said about my lying to you."

"What did you do?" she said. "Put a rush on the order? Is that why everyone was so busy this week?

Christmas toys; *that's* a hoot. What were *you* doing, trying it for size?"

"I honestly don't know what you're—"

"The dummy!" she said. She leaned toward him, holding the banister. "The robot! Oh very good; attorney surprised by a new allegation. You're wasting yourself in trusts and estates; you belong in a courtroom. What does it cost? Would you tell me? I'm dying to know. What's the going price for a stay-in-the- kitchen wife with big boobs and no demands? A fortune, I'll bet. Or do they do it dirt-cheap, out of that good old Men's Association spirit? And what happens to the real ones? The incinerator? Stepford Pond?"

He looked at her, standing with his hands to the wall and the banister. "Go upstairs and lie down," he said.

"I'm going out," she said.

He shook his head. "No," he said. "Not when you're talking like this. Go upstairs and rest."

She came down a step. "I'm not going to stay here to be—"

"*You're not going out,*" he said. "Now go up and rest. When you've calmed down we'll—try to talk sensibly."

She looked at him standing there with his hands to the wall and the banister, looked at her coat on the chair—and turned and went quickly up the stairs. She went into the bedroom and closed the door; turned the key, switched on the lights.

She went to the dresser, pulled a drawer open, and got out a bulky white sweater; shook it unfolded and thrust her arms in and sleeved them. She pulled the turtleneck down over her head and gathered her hair and drew it free. The door was tried, tapped on.

"Joanna?"

"Scram," she said, pulling the sweater down around her. "I'm resting. You told me to rest."

"Let me in for a minute."

She stood watching the door, said nothing.

"Joanna, unlock the door."

"Later," she said. "I want to be alone for a while."

She stood without moving, watching the door.

"All right. Later."

She stood and listened—to silence—and turned to the dresser and eased the top drawer open. She searched in it and found a pair of white gloves. She wriggled a hand into one and the other, and pulled out a long striped scarf and looped it around her neck.

She went to the door and listened, and switched the lights off.

She went to the window and raised the shade. The walk light shone. The Claybrooks' living room was lighted but empty; their upstairs windows were dark.

She raised the window sash quietly. The storm window stood behind it.

She'd forgot about the damn storm window.

She pushed at its bottom. It was tight, wouldn't budge. She hit at it with the side of her gloved fist, and pushed again with both hands. It gave, swinging outward a few inches—and would swing no farther. Small metal arms at its sides reached open to their fullest. She would have to unclamp them from the window frame.

Light fanned out on the snow below.

He was in the den.

She stood straight and listened; a tiny-toothed chittering came from behind her, from the phone on the night table; came again and again, long, short, long.

He was dialing the den phone.

Calling Dale Coba to tell him she was there. Proceed with plans. All systems go.

She tiptoed slowly to the door, listened, and turned the key back and eased the door open, a hand held against it. Pete's Star Trek gun lay by the threshold of his room. Walter's voice burred faintly.

She tiptoed to the stairs and started slowly, quietly down, pressing close to the wall, looking down through the banister supports at the corner of the den doorway.

". . . not sure I can handle her myself . . ."

You're goddamn right you can't, counselor.

But the chair by the front door was empty, her coat and handbag (car keys, wallet) gone.

Still, this was better than going through the window.

She made it down to the hall. He talked, and was quiet. Look for the handbag?

He moved in the den and she ducked into the living room, stood at the wall, her back pressing tight.

His footsteps came into the hall, came near the doorway, stopped.

She held her breath.

A string of short hisses—his usual let's-see-now

sound before tackling major projects; putting up
storm windows, assembling a tricycle. (Killing a
wife? Or did Coba the hunter perform that service?)
She closed her eyes and tried not to think, afraid her
thoughts would somehow beckon him.

His footsteps went up the stairs, slowly.

She opened her eyes and freed her breath bit by
bit, waiting as he went higher.

She hurried quietly across the living room, around
chairs, the lamp table; unlocked the door to the patio
and opened it, unlocked the storm door and pushed it
against a base of drifted snow.

She squeezed herself out and ran over snow, ran
and ran with her heart pounding; ran toward dark
tree trunks over snow that was sled-tracked, Pete-
and-Kim-boot-marked; ran, ran, and clutched a trunk
and swung around it and rushed-stumbled-groped
through tree trunks, tree trunks. She rushed, stum-
bled, groped, keeping to the center of the long belt of
trees that separated the houses on Fairview from the
houses on Harvest.

She had to get to Ruthanne's. Ruthanne would lend
her money and a coat, let her call an Eastbridge taxi
or someone in the city—Shep, Doris, Andreas—
someone with a car who would come pick her up.

Pete and Kim would be all right; she *had* to believe
that. They'd be all right till she got to the city and
spoke to people, spoke to a lawyer, got them back

from Walter. They were probably being cared for beautifully by Bobbie or Carol or Mary Ann Stavros —by the things that were called by those names, that is.

And Ruthanne had to be *warned*. Maybe they could go together—though Ruthanne had time yet.

She came to the end of the belt of trees, made sure no cars were coming, and ran across Winter Hill Drive. Snow-pillowed spruce trees lined the far side of it; she hurried along behind them, her arms folded across her chest, her hands in their thin gloves burrowed in her armpits.

Gwendolyn Lane, where Ruthanne lived, was somewhere near Short Ridge Hill, out past Bobbie's; getting there would take almost an hour. More, probably, with the snow on the ground and the darkness. And she didn't dare hitchhike because any car could be Walter, and she wouldn't know till too late.

Not only Walter, she realized suddenly. They would *all* be out looking for her, cruising the roads with flashlights, spotlights. How could they let her get away and tell? *Every* man was a threat, every car a danger. She would have to make sure Ruthanne's husband wasn't there before she rang the bell; look through the windows.

Oh God, *could* she get away? None of the others had.

But maybe none of the others had tried. Bobbie hadn't, Charmaine hadn't. Maybe she was the first one to find out in time. If it *was* in time . . .

She left Winter Hill and hurried down Talcott Lane. Headlights flashed, and a car swung from a driveway ahead on the other side. She crouched beside a parked car and froze, and light swam under her and the car drove past. She stood and looked: the car was going slowly, and sure enough, a spotlight beam lanced from it and slid a wobble of light over housefronts and lawns of snow.

She hurried down Talcott, past silent houses with Christmas-lighted windows and Christmas-light-trimmed doors. Her feet and legs were cold, but she was all right. At the end of Talcott was Old Norwood Road, and from there she would take either Chimney Road or Hunnicutt.

A dog barked nearby, barked ragingly; but the barking dropped behind her as she hurried on.

A black arm of tree branch lay on the trodden snow. She set her boot across it and broke off half of it, and hurried on, holding the cold wet strength of branch in her thin-gloved hand.

A flashlight gleamed in Pine Tree Lane. She ran between two houses, ran over snow toward a snow-dome of bush; huddled behind it panting, holding the branch tightly in her aching-cold hand.

She looked out—at the backs of houses, their windows alight. From the rooftop of one a stream of red sparks lofted and danced, dying among the stars.

The flashlight came swaying from between two houses, and she drew back behind the bush. She rubbed a stockinged knee, warmed the other in the crook of her elbow.

Wan light swept toward her over snow, and spots of light slid away over her skirt and gloved hand.

She waited, waited longer, and looked out. A dark man-shape went toward the houses, following a patch of lighted snow.

She waited till the man had gone, and rose and hurried toward the next street over. Hickory Lane? Switzer? She wasn't sure which it was, but both of them led toward Short Ridge Road.

Her feet were numb, despite the boots' fleece lining.

A light shone blindingly and she turned and ran. A light ahead swung toward her and she ran to the side, up a cleared driveway, past the side of a garage, and down a long slope of snow. She slipped and fell, clambered to her feet still holding the branch—the lights were bobbing toward her—and ran over level snow. A light swung toward her. She turned, toward snow with no hiding place, and turned, and stood where she was, panting. "Get away!" she cried at the lights bobbing toward her, two on one side, one on the other. She raised the branch. "Get away!"

Flashlights bobbed toward her, and slowed and stopped, their radiance blinding. "Get away!" she cried, and shielded her eyes.

The light lessened. "Put them out. We're not going

to hurt you, Mrs. Eberhart." "Don't be afraid. We're Walter's friends." The light went; she lowered her hand. "*Your* friends too. I'm Frank Roddenberry. You know me." "Take it easy, no one's going to hurt you."

Shapes darker than the darkness stood before her. "Stay away," she said, raising the branch higher.

"You don't need that."

"We're not going to hurt you."

"Then get away," she said.

"Everyone's out looking for you," Frank Roddenberry's voice said. "Walter's worried."

"I'll bet he is," she said.

They stood before her, four or five yards away; three men. "You shouldn't be running around like this, no coat on," one of them said.

"Get away," she said.

"P-put it down," Frank said. "No one's going to hurt you."

"Mrs. Eberhart, I was on the phone with Walter not five minutes ago." The man in the middle was speaking. "We know about this idea you've got. It's *wrong*, Mrs. Eberhart. Believe me, it's just not so."

"Nobody's making robots," Frank said.

"You must think we're a hell of a lot smarter than we really are," the man in the middle said. "Robots that can drive cars? And cook meals? And trim kids' hair?"

"And so real-looking that the kids wouldn't notice?" the third man said. He was short and wide.

"You must think we're a townful of geniuses," the man in the middle said. "Believe me, we're not."

"You're the men who put us on the moon," she said.

"*Who* is?" he said. "Not me. Frank, did you put anybody on the moon? Bernie?"

"Not me," Frank said.

The short man laughed. "Not me, Wynn," he said. "Not that I know of."

"I think you've got us mixed up with a couple of other fellows," the man in the middle said. "Leonardo da Vinci and Albert Einstein, maybe."

"My gosh," the short man said, "we don't want *robots* for wives. We want real women."

"Get away and let me go on," she said.

They stood there, darker than the darkness. "Joanna," Frank said, "if you were right and we could make robots that were so fantastic and lifelike, don't you think we'd cash in on it somehow?"

"That's right," the man in the middle said. "We could all be rich with that kind of know-how."

"Maybe you're going to," she said. "Maybe this is just the beginning."

"Oh my Lord," the man said, "you've got an answer for everything. *You* should have been the lawyer, not Walter."

Frank and the short man laughed.

"Come on, Joanna," Frank said, "p-put down that b-bat or whatever it is and—"

"Get away and let me go on!" she said.

"We can't do that," the man in the middle said. "You'll catch pneumonia. Or get hit by a car."

"I'm going to a friend's house," she said. "I'll inside in a few minutes. I'd be inside *now* if you hadn't—oh Jesus . . ." She lowered the branch and rubbed her arm; and rubbed her eyes and her forehead, shivering.

"Will you let us *prove* to you that you're wrong?" the man in the middle said. "Then we'll take you *home*, and you can get some help if you need it."

She looked at his dark shape. "*Prove* to me?" she said.

"We'll take you to the house, the Men's Association house—"

"Oh no."

"Now just a second; just hear me out please. We'll take you to the house and you can check it over from stem to stern. I'm sure nobody'll object, under the circumstances. And you'll see there's—"

"I'm not setting foot in—"

"You'll see there's no robot factory there," he said. "There's a bar and a card room and a few other rooms, and that's it. There's a projector and some very X-rated movies; that's our big secret."

"And the slot machines," the short man said.

"Yes. We've got some slot machines."

"I wouldn't set foot in there without an armed guard," she said. "Of women soldiers."

"We'll clear everyone out," Frank said. "You'll have the p-place all to yourself."

"I won't go," she said.

"Mrs. Eberhart," the man in the middle said, "we're trying to be as gentle about this as we know how, but there's a limit to how long we're going to stand here parleying."

"Wait a minute," the short man said, "I've got an

idea. Suppose one of these women you think is a
robot—suppose she was to cut herself on the finger,
and bleed. Would *that* convince you she was a real
person? Or would you say we made robots with
blood under the skin?"

"For God's sake, Bernie," the man in the middle
said, and Frank said, "You can't—ask someone to cut
herself just to—"

"Will you let her answer the question, please?
Well, Mrs. Eberhart? Would that convince you? If she
cut her finger and bled?"

"*Ber*nie . . ."

"Just let her answer, damn it!"

Joanna stood staring, and nodded. "If she bled,"
she said, "I would—think she was—real . . ."

"We're not going to ask someone to cut herself.
We're going to go to—"

"Bobbie would do it," she said. "If she's really
Bobbie. She's my friend. Bobbie Markowe."

"On Fox Hollow Lane?" the short man asked.

"Yes," she said.

"You see?" he said. "It's two minutes from here.
Just think for a second, will you? We won't have to go
all the way in to the Center; we won't have to make
Mrs. Eberhart go somewhere she doesn't want
to . . ."

Nobody said anything.

"I guess it's—not a b-bad idea," Frank said. "We
could speak to Mrs. Markowe . . ."

"She won't bleed," Joanna said.

"She will," the man in the middle said. "And when

she does, you'll know you're wrong and you'll let us take you home to Walter, without any arguments."

"*If* she does," she said. "Yes."

"All right," he said. "Frank, you run on ahead and see if she's there and explain to her. I'm going to leave my flashlight on the ground here, Mrs. Eberhart. Bernie and I'll go a little ahead, and you pick it up and follow us, as far behind as makes you comfortable. But keep the light on us so we know you're still there. I'm leaving my coat too; put it on. I can hear your teeth chattering."

She was wrong, she knew it. She was wrong and frozen and wet and tired and hungry, and pulled eighteen ways by conflicting demands. Including to pee.

If they were killers, they'd have killed her *then*. The branch wouldn't have stopped them, three men facing one woman.

She lifted the branch and looked at it, walking slowly, her feet aching. She let the branch fall. Her glove was wet and dirty, her fingers frozen. She flexed them, and tucked her hand into her other armpit. She held the long heavy flashlight as steadily as she could.

The men walked with small steps ahead of her. The short man wore a brown coat and a red leather cap; the taller man, a green shirt and tan pants tucked into brown boots. He had reddish-blond hair.

His sheepskin coat lay warm on her shoulders. Its smell was strong and good—of animals, of life.

Bobbie would bleed. It was coincidence that Dale Coba had worked on robots at Disneyland, that Claude Axhelm thought he was Henry Higgins, that Ike Mazzard drew his flattering sketches. Coincidence, that she had spun into—into madness. Yes, madness. ("It's *not* catastrophic," Dr. Fancher said, smiling. "I'm sure I can help you.")

Bobbie would bleed, and she would go home and get warm.

Home to Walter?

When had it begun, her distrust of him, the feeling of nothingness between them? Whose fault was it?

His face had grown fuller; why hadn't she noticed it before today? Had she been too busy taking pictures, working in the darkroom?

She would call Dr. Fancher on Monday, would go and lie on the brown leather couch; would cry a little maybe, and try to become happy.

The men waited at the corner of Fox Hollow Lane. She made herself walk faster.

Frank stood waiting in Bobbie's bright doorway. The men talked with him, and turned to her as she came slowly up the walk.

Frank smiled. "She says sure," he said. "If it'll make you feel b-better she'll be glad to do it."

She gave the flashlight to the green-shirted man. His face was broad and leathery, strong-looking. "We'll wait out here," he said, lifting the coat from her shoulders.

She said, "She doesn't have to . . ."

"No, go on," he said. "You'll only start wondering again later."

Frank came out onto the doorstep. "She's in the kitchen," he said.

She went into the house. Its warmth surrounded her. Rock music blared and thumped from upstairs.

She went down the hallway, flexing her aching hands.

Bobbie stood waiting in the kitchen, in red slacks and an apron with a big daisy on it. "Hi, Joanna," she said, and smiled. Beautiful bosomy Bobbie. But not a robot.

"Hi," she said. She held the doorjamb, and leaned to it and rested the side of her head against it.

"I'm sorry to hear you're in such a state," Bobbie said.

"Sorry to be in it," she said.

"I don't mind cutting my finger a little," Bobbie said, "if it'll ease your mind for you." She walked to a counter. Walked smoothly, steadily, gracefully. Opened a drawer.

"Bobbie . . ." Joanna said. She closed her eyes, and opened them. "Are you really Bobbie?" she asked.

"Of course I am," Bobbie said, a knife in her hand.

She went to the sink. "Come here," she said. "You can't see from there."

The rock music blared louder. "What's going on upstairs?" Joanna asked.

"I don't know," Bobbie said. "Dave has the boys up there. Come here. You can't see."

The knife was large, its blade pointed. "You'll amputate your whole hand with that thing," Joanna said.

"I'll be careful," Bobbie said, smiling. "Come on." She beckoned, holding the large knife.

Joanna raised her head from the jamb, and took her hand from it. She went into the kitchen—so shining and immaculate, so un-Bobbie-like.

She stopped. *The music is in case I scream*, she thought. *She isn't going to cut her finger; she's going to—*

"Come on," Bobbie said, standing by the sink, beckoning, holding the point-bladed knife.

Not catastrophic, Dr. Fancher? Thinking they're robots not women? Thinking Bobbie would kill me? Are you sure you can help me?

"You don't have to do it," she said to Bobbie.

"It'll ease your mind," Bobbie said.

"I'm seeing a shrink after New Year's," she said. *"That*'ll ease my mind. At least I hope it will."

"Come on," Bobbie said. "The men are waiting."

Joanna went forward, toward Bobbie standing by the sink with the knife in her hand, so real-looking—skin, eyes, hair, hands, rising-falling aproned bosom—that she *couldn't* be a robot, she simply *couldn't* be, and that was all there was to it.

·   ·   ·

The men stood on the doorstep, blowing out steamy breath, their hands deep in their pockets. Frank hipped from side to side with the beat of the loud rock music.

Bernie said, "What's taking so long?"

Wynn and Frank shrugged.

The rock music blared.

Wynn said, "I'm going to call Walter and tell him we found her." He went into the house.

"Get Dave's car keys!" Frank called after him.

3

The market parking lot was pretty well filled, but she found a good place up near the front; and that, plus the sun's warmth and the moist sweet smell of the air when she got out of the car, made her feel less bothered about having to be shopping. A *little* less bothered, anyway.

Miss Austrian came limping and caning toward her from the market's entrance, with a small paper bag in her hand and—she didn't believe it—a friendly smile on her Queen-of-Hearts white face. For her? "Good morning, Mrs. Hendry," Miss Austrian said.

What do you know, black is bearable. "Good morning," she said.

"March is certainly going out like a lamb, isn't it?"

"Yes," she said. "It seemed like it was going to be a two-headed lion."

Miss Austrian stopped and stood looking at her. "You haven't been in the library in months," she said. "I hope we haven't lost you to television."

"Oh no, not me," she said, smiling. "I've been working."

"On another book?"

"Yes."

"Good. Let me know when it's going to be published; we'll order a copy."

"I will," she said. "And I'll be in soon. I'm almost done with it."

"Have a good day," Miss Austrian said, smiling and caning away.

"Thanks. You too."

Well, there was *one* sale.

Maybe she'd been hypersensitive. Maybe Miss Austrian was cold to whites too until they'd been there a few months.

She went through the market's opening-by-themselves doors and found an empty cart. The aisles were the usual Saturday morning parade.

She went quickly, taking what she needed, maneuvering the cart in and out and around. "Excuse me. Excuse me, please." It still bugged her the way they shopped so languidly, gliding along as if they never sweated. How white could you get? Even filling their *carts* just so! She could shop the whole market in the time they did one aisle.

Joanna Eberhart came toward her, looking terrific in a tightly belted pale blue coat. She had a fine figure and was prettier than Ruthanne remembered, her dark hair gleaming in graceful drawn-back wings. She came along slowly, looking at the shelves.

"Hello, Joanna," Ruthanne said.

Joanna stopped and looked at her with thick-lashed brown eyes. "Ruthanne," she said, and smiled. "Hello. How are you?" Her bow lips were red, her complexion pale rose and perfect.

"I'm fine," Ruthanne said, smiling. "I don't have to ask how *you* are; you look marvelous."

"Thanks," Joanna said. "I've been taking better care of myself lately."

"It certainly shows," Ruthanne said.

"I'm sorry I haven't called you," Joanna said.

"Oh that's all right." Ruthanne hitched her cart over in front of Joanna's so people could get by them.

"I meant to," Joanna said, "but there's been so much to do around the house. You know how it is."

"That's all right," Ruthanne said. "I've been busy too. I'm almost done with my book. Just one more main drawing and a few small ones."

"Congratulations," Joanna said.

"Thanks," Ruthanne said. "What have *you* been up to? Have you taken any interesting pictures?"

"Oh no," Joanna said. "I don't do much photography any more."

"You don't?" Ruthanne said.

"No," Joanna said. "I wasn't especially talented, and I was wasting a lot of time I really have better uses for."

Ruthanne looked at her.

"I'll call you one of these days when I get caught up with things," Joanna said, smiling.

"What are you doing then, besides your housework?" Ruthanne asked her.

"Nothing, really," Joanna said. "Housework's enough for me. I used to feel I had to have other interests, but I'm more at ease with myself now. I'm much happier too, and so is my family. That's what counts, isn't it?"

"Yes, I guess so," Ruthanne said. She looked down at their carts, her own jumble-filled one against Joanna's neatly filled one. She hitched hers out of Joanna's way. "Maybe we can have that lunch," she said, looking at Joanna. "Now that I'm finishing the book."

"Maybe we can," Joanna said. "It was nice seeing you."

"Same here," Ruthanne said.

Joanna, smiling, walked away—and stopped, took a box from a shelf, looked at it, and fitted it down into her cart. She went away down the market aisle.

Ruthanne stood watching her, and turned and went on in the other direction.

She couldn't get to work. She paced and turned in the close-walled room; looked out the window at Chickie and Sara playing with the Cohane girls; leafed through the stack of finished drawings and found them not as amusing and skillful as she'd thought they were.

When she finally got going on Penny at the wheel of the *Bertha P. Moran*, it was practically five o'clock.

She went down to the den.

Royal sat reading *Men in Groups*, his feet in blue socks on the hassock. He looked up at her. "Done?" he asked. He had fixed the frame of his glasses with adhesive tape.

"Hell, no," she said. "I just got started."

"How come?"

"*I* don't know," she said. "*Something's* been bugging me. Listen, would you do me a favor? Now that it's moving I want to stay with it."

"Supper?" he said.

She nodded. "Would you take them to the pizza place? Or to McDonald's?"

He took his pipe from the table. "All right," he said.

"I want to get it done with," she said. "Otherwise I won't enjoy next weekend."

He laid the open book down across his lap and took his pipe-cleaning gadget from the table.

She turned to go, and looked back at him. "You sure you don't mind?" she asked.

He twisted the gadget back and forth in the pipe bowl. "Sure," he said. "Stay with it." He looked up at her and smiled. "I don't mind," he said.

Here is the first chapter of Ira Levin's new novel, SLIVER—his first book in thirteen years. It is a chiller that explores the menacing evil behind the glittering facades of New York City's high-tech, high-rise homes, and the dark possibilities inside each of us. The novel opens with deceptive quietness . . .

Chapter 1

IT WAS A GOOD good Monday morning to begin with—the Hoffmans slugging it out again, Dr. Palme on the phone with a suicidal expatient, the Coles' maid getting it off with one of their vibrators, Lesley and Phil meeting in the laundry room—and then it got even better. MacEvoy came into the lobby with a woman who looked like Thea Marshall, the same oval face, the same dark hair. Obviously she was there to look at 20B, repainted the week before.

He watched them ride up in the number-two elevator. She was beautifully built, tall and bosomy, in a good-looking medium-dark suit. Threw a glance his way then stood with a hand on her shoulder bag watching MacEvoy spieling about the central air conditioning and the Poggenpohl kitchen. Thirty-five or -six. A strong resemblance.

He put the 20B living room and bedroom on the masters and watched her come into the foyer and across the bare living room, her heels twanging on the parquet. She looked good from behind too as she went to the window and stood facing out over the lower buildings across Madison. "It *is* a glorious view," she said, and her voice, melodic and throaty, echoed Thea Marshall's.

He couldn't spot a wedding ring but she was probably married or living with someone. He was going to approve her no matter what, of course, assuming she decided she wanted the apartment. He crossed his fingers.

She turned from the window, looked around, smiled. Raised her face. Coming closer, she looked right at him—Thea Marshall looked right at him—knocking him breathless.

"What a lovely light," she said. The shallow glass ceiling dish was sculpted in Art Deco curves. In its chrome center her small raspberry-clad reflection hung face down looking at her.

"Isn't it?" Mrs. MacEvoy said, coming up beside her. "They're all through the building. Truly, no expense was spared. It was planned as a condo originally. The rent is a bargain, considering."

The rent was high but not impossible. She walked back toward the foyer, turned, surveyed the room—freshly white-painted, twenty by twenty-two, the window wide and large, the floor parquet, a pass-through to the kitchen. . . . If the rest of the apartment was on a par, she would have to make a decision then and there, first shot out of the classifieds. Did she *really* want to leave Bank Street? Go through all the hassle of moving?

She went on to the foyer.

The kitchen was handsome—tan laminate, stainless steel. Fluorescent lighting under the cabinets, appliances trim and foursquare. Good counter space.

The bathroom beyond it was glitzy but fun. Black glass walls, black fixtures, chrome hardware; a large tub, a stall shower. Tube lights by the over-the-sink cabinet; another chrome-centered Art Deco dish in the black glass ceiling, smaller than the once in the living room.

The bedroom, at the end of the foyer, was almost as large as the living room, freshly white too, the left-hand wall all accordiondoored closets. Another wide window at the back, another great view—a slice of the yellowing park and part of the reservoir, the roof of a Gothic mansion on Fifth. More than enough space for the desk against the right-hand wall by the window, with the bed, of course, across from the window and facing it. She sighed at her upside-down self in the ceiling light, at Mrs. MacEvoy waiting in the corner by the door. "This is the first apartment I've looked at," she said.

Mrs. MacEvoy smiled. "It's a gem," she said. "I wouldn't let it slip through my fingers."

They went back into the foyer. Mrs. MacEvoy opened the linen closet.

She took another look around, thinking about her beautiful apartment on Bank Street with its high ceilings and working fireplace. And its rock club on the corner, its roaches, its two years of Jeff and six years of Alex.

"I'll take it," she said.

Mrs. MacEvoy smiled. "Let's go back to my office," she said. "You can fill out the application and I'll put it right in the works."

He got antsy waiting for Edgar's call. It didn't come till late Wednesday afternoon. "Hello,

Edgar," he said, killing both masters, "how are you?"

"Getting on tolerably well. You?"

"Fine," he said.

"The September statement is on its way; considering how the market's been behaving, I think you'll be pleased. About the building: I had Mills speak to Dmitri again about the lobby."

"Tell him to try it in Russian," he said. "That piece of marble is still there. I mean those two pieces."

"I'm sure the new piece is on order, I'll check and get back to you. And Mrs. MacEvoy has an applicant for twenty B. Did I tell you it was going vacant?"

"Yes," he said, "you did."

"Kay Norris. Thirty-nine, divorced. She's a senior editor at Diadem, the publishing house, so she ought to be nice and quiet. Credit history and references first rate. Mrs. MacEvoy says she's good-looking. She has one cat."

"Is Kay her name or her initial?" he asked.

"Her name."

"Kay Norris."

"Yes."

Printing it on the clipboard, he said, "She sounds ideal. Tell Mills to see that everyone takes extra good care of her."

"I will. There's nothing else at the moment. . . ."

"Then don't let me keep you," he said. Hung up.

Underlined it: *Kay Norris.*

Older than he'd thought, thirty-nine.

Thea Marshall had been forty when she died; he drew a breath, sighed a long sigh.

He switched on the masters and put her living room on 1 and her bedroom on 2, the same as Monday morning. The bedroom glared, sunlight pouring through the bare window. He turned the brightness down. Up a little in the living room.

His hands on the console, he gazed at the two empty rooms on the twin masters. The monitors spread away in a multitiered wings, blue-white, flicking with movement here and there.

She called Alex on Thursday night and told him to come get his books.

"Oh God, Kay, I know I keep saying it but this is *really* the worst possible time, the semester starting. You'll have to keep them just a few more months."

"Sorry, I can't," she said. "I'm moving a week from tomorrow. Either pick them up or

I'm putting them outside. I've lost my interest in medieval architecture. God knows why."

He hadn't heard about her breakup with Jeff. He sounded genuinely sorry. "It's *good* you're moving, it's a fine idea. Start fresh. What have you found?"

She told him about it. "And it's on the next-to-the-top floor," she said. "You can see some of the East River from the living room and a piece of Central Park from the bedroom. Daylight galore. It's a lovely neighborhood, lots of well-kept old buildings, low ones, and the Cooper-Hewitt Museum is a block away."

"Thirteen. . .Hundred. . .Madison. . ."— in the musing tone he used before putting her down. "A sliver building? Narrow site?"

She drew breath and said, "Yes . . ."

"Kay, that's where the man was decapitated in the elevator machinery last winter. Remember? The super? There've been three or four deaths there and it's only a few years old. I remember thinking it's a pity the address is Thirteen Hundred because it reinforces superstition. That was the lead-in they used on TV, 'Thirteen hundred is an unlucky number on Madison Avenue' or some such. Of course you're—" "Alex," she said, "I knew about that. Do you think that *I'm* superstitious? Why did you expect me to mention it?"

"I was about to *say*, of course you're *not su-*

perstitious, but I thought you would want to know anyway, if you didn't."

"The books, Alex," she said.

They agreed he would come pack them on Sunday afternoon and have them removed during the week. They said good-by, she hung up.

Old Reliable. Negative, negative, negative.

It was awful about the super but the apartment was great nonetheless. She certainly wasn't going to let Alex and some tabloid-TV newscaster sour her on it. Three or four deaths over three years wasn't remarkable; two apartments on a floor meant forty altogether, with couples, probably, in most of them—sixty or seventy people. Without counting the turnover. And the staff.

Felice rubbed against her ankle. She picked her up, cradled her on her shoulder, nuzzled purring calico fur. Said, "Ooh Felice, are *you* in for a surprise! A whole new world. No more roaches to play with. Poor you. At least I hope not. You never know."

DON'T MISS
THESE CURRENT
Bantam Bestsellers

☐	28362	**COREY LANE** Norman Zollinger	$4.50
☐	27636	**PASSAGE TO QUIVIRA** Norman Zollinger	$4.50
☐	27759	**RIDER TO CIBOLA** Norman Zollinger	$3.95
☐	27811	**DOCTORS** Erich Segal	$5.95
☐	28179	**TREVAYNE** Robert Ludlum	$5.95
☐	27807	**PARTNERS** John Martel	$4.95
☐	28058	**EVA LUNA** Isabel Allende	$4.95
☐	27597	**THE BONFIRE OF THE VANITIES** Tom Wolfe	$5.95
☐	27510	**THE BUTCHER'S THEATER** Jonathan Kellerman	$4.95
☐	27800	**THE ICARUS AGENDA** Robert Ludlum	$5.95
☐	27891	**PEOPLE LIKE US** Dominick Dunne	$4.95
☐	27953	**TO BE THE BEST** Barbara Taylor Bradford	$5.95
☐	26892	**THE GREAT SANTINI** Pat Conroy	$5.95
☐	26574	**SACRED SINS** Nora Roberts	$3.95
☐	28436	**PAYMENT IN BLOOD** Elizabeth George	$4.95
☐	28855	**THE WIND DANCER** Iris Johansen	$4.95
☐	28773	**THE BOURNE ULTIMATUM** Robert Ludlum	$5.95

Buy them at your local bookstore or use this page to order.